A Captain Hook, Crocodile,
& Wendy Darling Reimagining

DEVOUR THE SNAKE

NIKKI ST. CROWE

Cover Design by Emily Wittig Design

CONTENT WARNING

Graphic language, violence, abusive parent, verbally abusive parent/parent who uses derogatory language towards child, internal struggles with sexual identity/internal struggle of self due to parental abuse, graphic sexual content, mentions of spousal coma/death, blood drinking, captive/captivity, submission, talk of suicide, war, death of family

For a more comprehensive list of all of Nikki's work, please visit her website below.

https://www.nikkistcrowe.com/content-warnings

ACKNOWLEDGMENTS

This series would not be possible without the help of several people.

First and foremost, thank you to Jeff for sensitivity reading Devourer of Men and the relationship between James Hook and the Crocodile.

A huge thank you to Kylie @kylies.booknook for sensitivity reading for Asha and beta reading Devour the Snake!

I will be forever grateful for helping me to accurately and respectfully portray these characters. Any mistakes or inaccuracies that remain in this series are entirely my own.

I also want to thank you, the reader, for showing up for the Lost Boys and James, Roc, and Wendy again and again. I know how lucky I am.

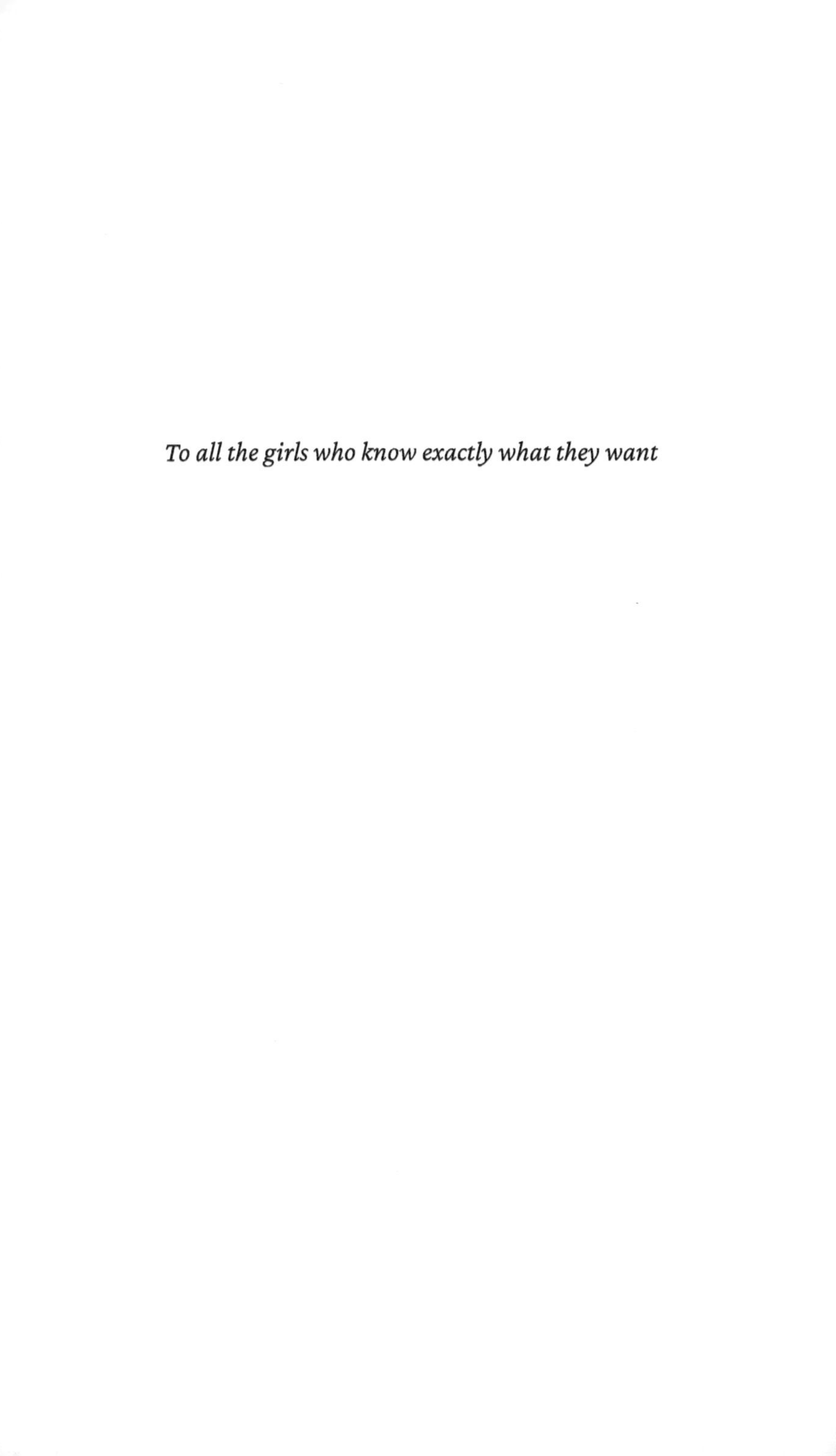

To all the girls who know exactly what they want

CHAPTER ONE
HOOK

A HAND-PAINTED MAP OF THE SEVEN ISLES SPANS THE ENTIRE BACK wall of the Portage Hall.

Winterland at the northwestern edge, the biggest island by far, dominating the sea, with its snowcapped mountains the farthest north. Next is Darkland, the second largest, with all of its many ports. Followed by Neverland, Everland, Summerland and Pleasureland across the rest of the map, the land masses slowly making their way south. Lostland is nowhere to be found, of course. It exists somewhere, but none of us know how to reach it.

We're currently discussing reports of a pod of sirens just off the coast of Summerland. Years and years ago, Smee and I found ourselves surrounded by sirens at the very beginning of their mating season. Thankfully, we'd been warned by one of the anthropological experts on Summerland and had hired a lute player who played his music nonstop while we skirted their territory.

We'd been warned that had we been just a few weeks later, no amount of music would have fought them off.

And thinking of Smee now makes my head hurt.

I haven't spoken to her since I left Neverland the first time.

I don't think I've ever gone this long without seeing her.

Sometimes I find myself absently turning to her, as if she's there in the room with me and then my heart sinks when I remember she's not.

We were always together and I realize now that I took her presence for granted.

"Time is always of the essence," Yal Mertz says. "We stay the course."

He's the Darkland Portage Minister, in charge of all importing and exporting. I met him a few weeks back when I wandered into the Portage Hall out of curiosity. It's hard to keep me out of the places where ships are discussed.

"You're in the middle of the siren mating season," I argue. "You need to shift the shipping lanes farther north if you want any ships to return."

As the minister, Yal is responsible for all charts and schedules. Not knowing the mating seasons of all the sea creatures is not only poor form, it's downright irresponsible. How he's made it this far in the job, I'll never know. If I wasn't concerned about being labeled a nepo boyfriend, I'd call for his firing. Some of the men are already whispering about the amount of influence I have in the Merchant District, considering I've only been on Darkland a little over two months.

But I have experience. Real fucking experience! Who cares who I'm sleeping with?

Though I will admit, fucking the future king of Darkland is a potential conflict of interest.

It's not like I'm being paid for my work, though.

"I've never seen sirens in the Loarring Strait," Yal

argues. "How do we know they aren't being controlled by...*someone*?"

The way he says this leads me to believe he's insinuating it's *someone* in particular. The Loarring Strait is not far off of where Lostland is supposed to be and rumors have started to swirl about my connection to the Myths, despite the fact I'm very clearly a victim of their meddling, not an ally.

I haven't been able to confirm it, but I think the Myth Makers were already planting rumors before Roc, Wendy, and I arrived here. Rumors that I have Myth Maker blood coursing through my veins. Never mind the fact that it was a Myth that was trying to take control of Roc's body, install him as king, and overthrow the Darkland court. Technically, they should be thanking us for saving them. Otherwise, they'd all be living under a Myth Maker banner right now.

"How does one control a siren?"

The voice rings out over the Portage Hall, cutting through the noise of us arguing.

Hearing the Crocodile makes the hair lift on the back of my neck.

Will I ever grow accustomed to him? To the way he smells, the way he feels, the way he sounds?

We all turn to the open double doors to Roc standing in a slant of sunlight, hands in his pockets, a cigarette dangling from the corner of his mouth.

He's wearing a black shirt, the sleeves rolled up to his elbows, revealing all the swirls of black ink on his pale skin.

The room goes silent.

All breath is held.

Roc takes a hit from the cigarette as he walks forward, then pinches the end between his thumb and index finger, pulling it out so he can exhale as he comes to a stop in front of Yal Mertz.

The smoke billows around the man.

Yal winces.

"Tell me, minister," Roc goes on. "If you can control a siren, I'd very much like to know how."

"Well...I don't know...me personally...I'm sure there are *ways.*"

"Mmmm." Roc looks at the map and the second his gaze is off Yal, the minister exhales with relief.

"How much time do we lose if we move the shipping lanes farther north?" Roc asks.

Yal looks at some of his men. The one with dark, wavy hair, Manuel I think his name is, whispers to his desk mate. They nod. Then Manuel says, "Fourteen hours, give or take."

Roc takes another hit, blows out another jet stream of smoke. "So would you rather lose twenty-eight hours or your life?" This, directed at the minister.

Yal's nostrils flare. He blinks in quick succession. "Twenty-eight hours for every trip, over the course of the season, amounts to the loss of several thousand dukets and we—"

"Then you helm the ship."

I'm watching Roc and Yal, but I sense the widening of eyes around us, the silence hanging on every word spoken.

"Uhhh...Your Grace?" Yal says.

"If you're so concerned with money," Roc says, "then you helm the ship. Take it through the Strait. Do not deviate."

"But...I...*we should*—"

Roc closes the last few feet between them. Because he

has a half foot of height on the minister, he makes a show of ducking down, putting his line of sight level with Yal's.

But the minister is looking everywhere but at Roc. "I apologize, Your Grace," he stutters. "I'll adjust the lanes and—"

"Do. *Not*. Deviate."

Yal swallows so loudly I think the next room hears.

"Very well."

"Good." Roc steps back and the tension immediately fades. "Captain?" he calls and turns for the door.

I don't know why I feel bad for Yal. If he follows Roc's orders, he'll be dead soon, lured from his ship by a siren. It's impossible to escape the call once it's on the wind.

But Christ, he should have known better. Roc is...well, *Roc*, and now he's a duke, soon to be king. It's one thing to disagree with a ruler, but to argue with him? Just to defend your pride?

Poor form, indeed.

I follow Roc out of the Portage Hall. We pass several pages filing paperwork in the annex, and two clerks in the front.

Everywhere Roc goes, he is watched. Watched and ogled and fawned over. I've always wondered how he does it, how he allows himself to be perceived at every turn without running from it.

I think that's why I took to pirating so well—people don't fawn over pirates. They run from them.

One of the pages drops several files when she bumps into a cabinet. In the outer office, both clerks whisper to one another while Roc holds the door for me.

"Have a good day, Your Grace!" the young man calls.

"Yes. A wonderful day!" the woman adds.

"It is promising to be a good *and* wonderful day," Roc

says back, and the clerks turn to one another and giggle into their hands.

As soon as we're outside beneath the barreled roof of the Portage Hall, I give Roc a shove.

"What?" he says to me, smiling, his teeth flashing. He knows what. He fucking knows.

"First of all, you've just sentenced that man to death."

"Oh. Pity for him." He makes his way down the marble steps. "He should have listened to you. Why you let him dismiss you is truly a mystery."

"I'm not in charge here. And you must know what they're saying."

"No. I don't." He's still smiling, like *yes, he does know what they are saying.*

"I don't want them thinking I've slept my way to the top."

"Oh, no. We can't have that."

"Stop smiling at me. Where are we going, anyway?"

We step into the street.

"Would you prefer I scowl at you instead?" he asks, ignoring my question.

The joy drops from his expression and is replaced with a brooding scowl that sharpens the lines of his face, and makes him ten times more attractive in a fucking instant.

My stomach dips. My cock takes notice.

"No. Stop that, too!"

He laughs. "I can't win with you, Captain. I'm just trying to have a good and wonderful day."

I grumble. "I must be a glutton for punishment to endure this torture."

He reaches over, grabs me by the back of the neck and hauls me close, his mouth at the shell of my ear. "The way you choked on my cock last night says yes, *glutton indeed.*"

"Bloody hell," I mutter as he steps away and smiles at a passerby as if he did not just whisper filthy things into my ear, leaving me flushed and hard.

2

THE CROCODILE BRINGS ME TO A CLIFF OVERLOOKING THE MAIN port of Darkland. It's a sunny day, the weather warm, the breeze enough to tousle his hair.

He lights another cigarette and stops at the cliff's edge. Beyond him, smoke billows up from the Factory District, while the sunlight burnishes the coast, and all of its little shops and houses, in swathes of gold and yellow.

It's a romantic spot.

I eye him, wondering what has brought him here, and why he's brought me.

Last night notwithstanding, Wendy and I have barely seen him these last two months. He's spent it assembling a council, then filing all of the paperwork to reclaim his title. He was finally awarded Duke of Maddred two weeks ago, then he and his council quickly turned to the business of claiming the throne.

He's to be crowned soon.

Now, the coronation planning has dominated his time and his attention, leaving me and Wendy to entertain ourselves. Wendy, it turns out, has found joy in healing others and volunteers at the hospital when she's able. I've found use for myself in the Merchant District, helping to plot shipping lines and better organize the harbor schedules.

Some nights, while I lie in bed with Wendy in my arms, while Roc burns the midnight oil in the office attached to our room, I have to poke myself with the sharp tine of my hook just to remind myself that it's all real.

At any given moment, I expect it all to pop like a bubble, that voice in the back of my mind trying to convince me that I still don't deserve it.

"I want to tell you something," Roc says after he blows out a breath of smoke.

"Okay."

"I've asked Wendy to marry me."

The air catches in my throat and then my mouth is dry, my tongue thick.

I'm panicking. Even though I don't have all of the information. This doesn't mean what I think it means...

Maybe this is it. Maybe the bubble is about to burst.

"Oh," I hear myself say. "What did she say?"

"She said yes, of course. Do you blame her? I'm rather handsome and charming."

I snort. "I loathe the moment that crown sits atop your head. Your ego will be insufferable."

"I do believe I warned you, Captain."

"So you did."

He takes another hit. When he exhales next, he says, "I would like to ask you the same."

I frown at him. "Ask me...what, exactly?"

"Marry me, Captain."

It pulls me to a stop. "What?"

He smiles. I think he's amused by my surprise and by his ability to still catch me off guard. "Marry me," he repeats.

"But...what about Wendy?"

"What about her?"

"You...you can't marry both—"

"Says who? I'm to be king. I marry who I want. If I say I

want to marry a bratty pirate captain and a Darling girl, then I will marry both."

I scoff. "You're teasing me."

The smile slips from his face. "I'm not."

"We...you...*you* hate commitment. What if you grow bored? What if—"

"Do you want me to beg, Captain? Do you want me to get down on one knee and declare my love for you? Because I will. If that's what you want."

"I would never ask you to do something you didn't want to do."

He laughs and takes a final hit of his cigarette before dropping it to the uneven rocky slope, crushing the ember beneath his boot. The wind swoops in, carrying several embers on a draft, and the bright gold swirls around him.

Even now, when I've had all of him, his body, his soul, his secrets, when I've witnessed him at his worst and seen him vulnerable, I'm still overwhelmed by his power and his beauty.

He is a dark storm that cannot be contained. The only option is to brace for the force of him and pray you survive to the other side.

And so I am always braced. Holding on for dear life.

He takes a step toward me, then crouches down onto one knee.

My stomach sways, the earth shifting like water beneath me.

He turns his head up and squints against the sunlight. His eyes, that liquid green, glint in the light.

"Will you marry me, James?"

My heart races in my ears and my eyes are burning even though I will not cry.

He used my name. He never calls me by my name. Names are a sore spot for him, his the sorest of all.

Will you marry me, James?

I know I love him. Maybe deep down, I always knew.

But it hits me now, *especially now*. Hits me like a gale force, and threatens to buckle my knees.

I love him in a way that feels a little reckless and violent.

If the ocean tried to steal him from me, I would declare war on it. When the sun pools at his feet, I am loathe to steal its place.

I am terrified of how much I love him.

How every hour of his absence feels hollow and dark.

I can't imagine one single moment without him by my side.

"Yes."

The wind almost swallows the word.

But of course, he hears it.

When he looks up at me again, dark hair windblown, the smile returns.

"Good," he tells me and then he rises to his full height, closes the distance between us, and pulls my mouth to his.

CHAPTER TWO
WENDY

"Ms. Darling?"

I look up from the pages of my book to find Hagan filling up the doorway of the library.

Roc hired Hagan as the house manager a month ago, but I think they are pretending she's a manager when really she's a bodyguard, mostly for me.

Hagan is taller than James, nearly as tall as Roc, but she surpasses both men in size. Her shoulders are broad, her thighs thick and muscular. Her dark hair is cut short, just below her ears, and is usually slicked back out of her face. She wears no makeup most days and her clothing is simple and expertly tailored to fit her body.

Whenever I cross paths with her in the house, I get the distinct impression she would be much happier on horseback with a sword in her hand, gutting anyone who dares get in her way.

I guess I shouldn't be surprised—Roc loves women who are regularly underestimated or dismissed, and while I can spot Hagan's efficiency easily, I would bet my fortune on the fact that men constantly overlook her.

"Yes?" I say.

"Captain Hook has returned to the manor."

I leap out of the divan, the one made of crushed velvet the color of blushing roses. James picked it out for me when he and Roc were furnishing the manor. James has an eye for elegant things. In some ways, I think he and Roc appreciate decadence far more than I do. But I will also gladly indulge in what they gift me. Maddred Manor is quickly filling up with beautiful things. Day by day, it's starting to feel more like a home. *Our home.*

"Is he in the house yet?" I ask, making my way to the door.

"He was walking up the front lawn when I spotted him."

I hurry past Hagan. "Did he look happy?"

"He looked…"

She follows behind me.

I stop at the bend in the next hallway to glance back at her.

"Yes," she decides. "He looked happy."

The smile that spreads over my face is involuntary. Likely too big, a bit maniacal. I clap like a child at the circus. "He said yes. He must have said yes!"

"It would seem so," Hagan answers as I hurry away.

Because Asha has been busy at the Darkland Archives, and James has been busy at the Portage Hall, and Roc has just been plain busy, Hagan is the only one I've been able to chat with. She knows all about the proposal. She isn't showing it, but I think she's just as invested in this outcome as I am.

I hear the door shut at the front of the house and pick up my pace so I don't lose James in the maze of corridors.

When Roc proposed to me, my first thought was absolutely not.

Not only did I not want an imbalance in our three-way relationship, I was in no hurry to submit to another husband.

But Roc convinced me that this time, it would be different.

Crown or not, I would not be required to submit to him. My freedom was mine to use as I pleased.

And furthermore, he intended to propose to James as well.

A three-way union was unconventional, but everything about Roc is unconventional. Why not his marriage?

Gathering my skirts so I don't trip, I hurry into the foyer and find James handing his coat to one of the servants.

"Did he ask you?" I blurt the words out before I can think better of it. Because what if he didn't? What if he didn't have the chance and now I've just blown the surprise?

James goes still. His arms hang at his sides, his thumb fidgeting, rubbing circles over the curve of his index finger. His hook flashes in the sunlight.

"He…"

"Yes?"

"I…"

"James!"

"Yes," he answers and exhales in a rush. "He asked me."

"And?"

"I said yes."

I leap at him. He catches me around the waist and lifts me off my feet, twirling me in the foyer. I cling to him, arms wrapped around his neck. We're giggling like fools but I wouldn't have it any other way.

James and I have a lot of time to make up for. Our pasts are filled with denial, rejection, failure, trauma and pain.

I want our future to be full of joy and celebration. And yes, giggling.

When he sets me down, I catch a flicker in his eyes.

"You're glowing," I observe.

He blushes, but doesn't deny it. "The Crocodile has that effect on us, does he not?"

I nod. "I still can't believe he's ours."

James sighs and rubs at the line of his brow. "Everyone in Darkland wants a piece of him..."

"And yet, it's you and I he returns to night after night."

James's gaze goes distant.

"What is it?" I ask.

He looks back at me. "What if I don't deserve it?"

I take his hand in mine and squeeze. "Oh, James. But what if you do?"

CHAPTER THREE
ROC

Punctual as always, Hagan appears in the doorway to my office a quarter past midnight. I've been home for less than ten minutes, but to Hagan, my quiet time doesn't matter as much as the day's debriefing. Her tasks are always an itch that must be scratched.

"Are you ready for me?" she asks.

I fetch a cigarette from my silver case and pop it into my mouth. "Yes, come in."

She enters my office and closes the door behind her, then crosses the room to one of the chairs in front of my desk.

I still find it annoying that I have not one, but two desks where papers and business and other equally important yet insufferably urgent items gather like flies on a corpse. Who would have known running a country would require so much fucking paperwork?

Hagan clasps her hands in her lap and waits.

Though she's always awake before I am and still awake long after I return home, there is no hint of exhaustion on her pale face. Her big, round eyes are as alert as ever.

I strike a match on the nearby striker box and the room fills with the burn of sulphur. I bring the small flame to the cigarette and inhale. The tobacco crackles and ignites. I lean back into my chair and give Hagan a flick of my finger, letting her know I'm ready.

When I started looking for a bodyguard for Wendy, I began my search by looking for an ex-guard or a semi-retired assassin from Winterland. The northern island makes some of the best murderers. During training, they're subjected to rough terrain and even worse weather. If snow and mountains won't stop them, a few thieves pose no risk at all.

But once word spread that I was looking to hire, Hagan appeared on my doorstep.

She sunk to a knee and held out her hand. In it was a gold pendant with a suit of clubs stamped in the center.

"Why did you leave Wonderland?" I asked her, not bothering to hide the thread of suspicion in my voice.

Clubs are soldiers, trained from the day they are born, meant only to serve the Queen of Hearts.

I'm not exactly on the queen's good side. Jabberwockies are the only thing in Wonderland that the queen could never control. It's why she hunted us, tried to kill us, failed and pivoted. She eventually found a loophole. She called it "murdering the time." But it's just a fucking curse. A horrible one, though.

Our uncle, the Madd Hatter, suffers from the murdering of time. Time abandoned him, trapping him at 6:00 P.M., forever desiring blood and unable to shift. The only thing worse than being a monster is being a monster with no route to your power.

Head still bowed, Hagan answered, "It's been a long

time since you've been to Wonderland and much has changed."

"Are the Clubs still loyal to the Hearts?"

"Some are. Some aren't."

"And you?"

She finally looked up. "If I come face to face with the queen again, I will carve out *her* heart."

A very small part of me wanted to ask about Alice next, but I decided that was an itch I couldn't scratch.

I hired Hagan on the spot. Clubs are good at their jobs because they are unassuming, and yet when it comes time to fight, they are some of the fiercest.

Now, Hagan sits across from me and details Wendy's movements for the day. I haven't explicitly told Wendy what Hagan's true role is, but I suspect if she found out I'm having her watched, she'd be pissed, followed immediately by flattery.

She doesn't like to be taken care of and yet it's what she desires most of all.

She's been spending more and more time at the clinic, but today she took the day off, knowing I was proposing to the Captain.

"There was nothing out of the ordinary," Hagan finishes. "I did find a few children trying to sneak in through the garden, but I scared them off."

"With sword or dagger?"

Hagan frowns. "My face."

I snort. "You do have a fearsome scowl."

"I do. Yes. Thank you."

"If that's all then..." I take another hit of my cigarette and lean back in my desk chair.

"There is one more thing."

I exhale and the smoke billows toward the ceiling. "I'm listening."

"I know it's not my place, but perhaps it would be in everyone's best interest if Captain Hook also had a guard?"

When I sit forward abruptly, the chair lets out a loud thunk. "Why? Did something happen?"

"No. It's just...he is as equally important to you?"

"Yes."

"Then why not protect him too?"

I sigh and rub at my eyes. "Normally, I would agree with you, but the Captain will notice someone tailing him, and then I will have to deal with his bratty attitude for weeks, and I don't really relish the idea. I'm very tired." If he knew I was doubting his capabilities, he'd give me the silent treatment and then I would have to beg him for just one fucking word.

I'm finding that the further I descend into running this country, the more I need him and Wendy.

I don't trust very many people here, and the Captain and Wendy are the two I trust the most.

I take another hit and exhale, elbows on my desktop as I think. Should I hire a guard for him? I do have spies in Darkland and I haven't heard anything yet. "Let's hold off for now," I decide. "But you'll let me know if I need to start worrying?"

"Yes. Of course."

The Captain isn't exactly making friends in Darkland, but most everyone who matters knows he's mine. They wouldn't fucking dare lay a hand on him.

"Thank you, Hagan. You're dismissed."

She rises to her feet, gives me a shallow bow, and then slips from the room.

For a woman her size, she's ridiculously graceful, nearly

silent. I wish I had two Hagans, one for Wendy and one for the Captain. But surely he can handle himself in a moment of danger?

No, he'll be fine. He's gotten this far without getting himself killed.

CHAPTER FOUR
WENDY

It's nearly one in the morning when I hear footsteps approaching my bathroom.

At this point, I've come to know the difference between James's footsteps and Roc's. They both move with purpose and confidence, but Roc's gait is slower, a bit more self-assured, as if he's in no hurry to get to where he's going, as if he knows people will wait regardless of the hour.

Now as Duke of Maddred and the future King of Darkland, there is always someone waiting for him. I've tried to occupy myself so I'm not just one more person in a crowd hoping for his attention.

And yet I am always coiled up, eager for him to appear, his eyes only on me.

The door opens and I inhale.

Butterflies war in my stomach.

I'm no better than the lot of them.

The moment he is near me, I'm buzzing with anticipation.

"Wendy Darling," he says and leans his shoulder into the door frame, crosses one foot over the other ankle. His gaze stretches over my naked body in the opaque water of my clawfoot tub. I added bubble bath, but that was over a half hour ago and the bubbles have popped.

"I missed you," I tell him.

He comes over to the tub and fetches the wooden stool tucked beneath my vanity. He sits by my side, his back propped against the wall.

"I missed you, too." He tips his head back and the crocodile mouth tattooed over his throat widens its jaws. "Where is our Captain?"

"Cleaning his guns."

He tsks. "He hasn't shot a man in months and yet every day…"

"I think it calms him."

"I suppose it does." He pulls out a cigarette and lights it. The smoke ribbons around his face.

He hasn't touched me, hasn't hinted at touching me, and yet I feel like he is all over me and I am pulsing with need.

Every time Roc enters a room, my veins sizzle and pop.

"He said yes," I say.

"He said yes." Roc exhales smoke. "How did he seem when he returned home?"

"Shocked."

Roc sits forward, elbows on his knees and starts cuffing the sleeve of his white button-up shirt. "In what way?"

"I think we both sometimes worry you'll run away."

He doesn't react to the confession. He curls his finger over the end of his cigarette and takes a long pull from it. The hot ember eats away at the rolled paper and the tobacco burns and burns as he watches me.

It's no secret that James and I doubt ourselves. That we question our luck. We have the infamous Devourer of Men in our bed. Everyone wants him. Including those who hate him. It's not just that he's handsome beyond measure. There's more to Roc than just his beautiful face and glorious body. There is a magnetism that almost feels holy. He's about to rule one of the wealthiest, most powerful islands in the Seven Isles and yet he seems like he cares very little for the power. Which makes him instantly ten times hotter for it.

A man who doesn't need more power and yet somehow gains it, is a man who automatically commands respect.

Roc slides off the stool and crouches by the bathtub. He puts his cigarette between his lips and grabs the nearby washcloth hanging over the edge of the tub. He gets the cloth wet and runs it down the bend of my knee.

"Did he seem happy?"

As he leans forward, his hand slipping beneath the surface of the water to reach my calf, a lock of his black hair falls in front of his eyes.

"Yes."

"And you?"

The cloth comes back up, passes my knee, then moves down my inner thigh.

A breath hitches in my throat.

"You make me happy, every day, every minute."

The end of the washcloth trails between my legs, just the faint tickle of it on my clit sends my vision spinning.

"Even when I'm gone for hours and hours?"

"Even then."

He moves to my other leg following the same pattern. Down to my calf, then up to my knee.

"Do I wish you were home more? Yes. But you are to be king. I know the life of a monarch. I know how to navigate it."

He takes another hit from the cigarette dangling from his mouth and then passes the cloth over my belly, missing my pussy on purpose.

I almost groan with need.

"The Captain doesn't," he points out.

"I'm sure we can occupy ourselves in your absence." I give him a coy smile but there is anguish in his gaze. "I'm sorry...I didn't mean..."

"Shhh." He trails the cloth over my exposed nipples and despite the warmth of the water, they bead beneath his attention. "I don't want to talk about the things I miss."

I nod, happy to take his commands as he slips the cloth beneath the water again and gently cleans my most sensitive area.

A gasp crawls out of me and I close my eyes and clutch at the sides of the tub.

Roc abandons the cloth and slips in further, the water past his elbow as he slides his fingers down my center, then two fingers inside of me.

I moan out, squirming for more, more, *more*.

The cigarette drops from Roc's mouth and hits the water with a hiss.

He grabs me by the throat with one hand holding me in place, while the other stays below the water playing with my pussy.

He fucks me with several fingers while circling my clit with his thumb.

"Sometimes when I'm in my office all alone, I think about you and the moans you make when I'm inside of you."

His grip on my throat tightens as my breathing quickens.

"Most days I'm stuck in the office, I spend half the hours hard just thinking about you writhing beneath me."

His words send liquid heat cascading down my belly, swelling in my clit. Every brush of his thumb is like lightning striking the earth—everything below trembles for release.

"Roc," I breathe out.

"Shhh," he says again, and his hand leaves my throat, comes up to my mouth. His thumb pushes past my lips and slides over the pad of my tongue. "Shut the fuck up, Wendy, and come for me."

I let all the tension melt from my bones until I am nothing but pliable flesh beneath Roc's attention.

He's doing his job beneath the water, sinking his fingers deeper, the pads of his fingertips hitting that hard ridge inside of me while his thumb circles my clit.

The pressure swells up, thumps against my rib cage, drums in my ears.

I want to please him more than I've ever wanted anything.

When he pops his thumb out of my mouth and uses the wet pad to rub at my exposed nipple, the pleasure escalates like a landslide.

The orgasm wrenches out of me in jittering waves.

The water sloshes against the edges of the tub as I jolt beneath the surface, and Roc rides through it with me, his arm locked between my legs. The press and release of his thumb is timed to the aftershocks that rock through me, squeezing out every last drop of the orgasm.

I twitch, breathe out.

When I finally open my eyes, Roc is just looking at me, taking in the sight of me, fucked and spent in the tub.

"Why would I ever run away from this?"

The question hangs between us.

He smiles, and it's laced with pride, because he knows he just treated me like the queen I once was and am destined to become again.

I feel satiated and happy and for once, content.

"I love you," I say, the words barely more than a whisper.

"I love you, too." He bends down and kisses me, teasing me with a quick slide of his tongue. "I'm going to find the Captain and we're all going to bed together for once." He straightens, letting the water drip from his arm. "That's an order."

I demure. "Yes, Your Grace."

He smiles, all teeth, and leaves me to get ready for bed.

CHAPTER FIVE
HOOK

My office in Maddred Manor is arranged precisely how I like it.

And yet, every night I find myself here, rearranging the pens, the papers, the bottles of oil I use to clean my guns.

It's a ritual I can't seem to unlock and tuck away.

I am resigned to it. But it's exhausting.

I'm just folding up the cleaning cloth I use for my pistols when Roc comes in.

His shirtsleeves are rolled up to his elbow, but the left sleeve is soaked nearly up to his shoulder.

I frown at him.

"Wendy was in the bath," he explains.

"Ahhh," I say.

He drops into the leather chair in front of my desk. For the first time in a long time, he looks exhausted.

"Will you make me a promise?"

I open my desk drawer and set the cloth in its place in front. "Depends on what the promise is."

"Be careful," he says.

"Is that the promise?"

"Just..." He sighs and scrubs at his face. "You have a mouth you love to run and if I found out you were using your mouth to get in trouble instead of using your mouth to please me, I would be in a very bad mood."

I roll my eyes. "I do not love to run my mouth."

"You do, Captain. It's my favorite thing about you. So long as it's aimed at me and not the hundreds of enemies I've made in the last month."

"Then stop making enemies."

"You try running a country and pleasing everyone beneath your purview. Just promise me."

"Fine. I will not run my mouth."

"Good." He stands and comes around the desk. "Hagan suggested I place a guard on you."

"She's Wendy's watchdog, isn't she?" He doesn't answer me, which is all the confirmation I need. "I knew it." He grabs me by the hips and walks me back until I bump into the bookcases. "I don't need a babysitter."

"I know," he says and the pressure of his grip tightens. "I told Hagan no."

"Really?"

"You sound surprised."

"You like to get your way."

"Yes, I do." He kisses me, slow and languidly, as if we have all the time in the world. "But if you disobey me, I will have no choice."

There are two sides of me: the side that likes to be in control and the side that likes for Roc to be in control. And both those sides chafe against one another, but sometimes they are one.

I can feel the hard length of him against my thigh.

If anyone, at any time, ordered me around, I would shoot them.

But when Roc does it...

I'm caged by him against the bookcases, commanded by him and yet there is no place I would rather be.

He can order me on my knees and I would plant myself on the floor.

"Fine," I mutter. "I will behave."

"Good boy, Captain."

I huff out a breath, and suddenly we're in a frenzy. His belt comes off with a snap and I unbutton my pants, shoving them down.

He spins me around, bends me over my desk.

Like a lever pulled, I'm compliant beneath him. His fingers thread through my hair and pull my head back, exposing my neck. He kisses up my throat, licks the beat of my heart until he reaches the stubble along my jaw.

Our frantic movements send the pens rolling, the papers flying.

But I don't care.

I don't fucking care.

And because we've fucked in here a dozen times already, he knows where I keep the lube.

The jar is out and uncorked within seconds and the hot, wet slide of it on my ass sends my cock throbbing just below the edge of the desk.

"Have I told you, Captain, how much I love your ass?"

I groan into the desk. "Tell me again."

The blunt head of his cock slips against the lube, teasing my opening.

"I love your fucking ass."

He adjusts his hips, lining himself up.

"I've been thinking about your ass all fucking day. You and Wendy torment my thoughts and all I can think about is being home with you."

Then he pushes inside and I let out a low, agonizing moan of pleasure as he stretches me open.

"Fuck," I mutter, gripping the edge of the desk with one hand while my hook gouges the wood top.

Roc throbs inside of me, relentless with his pursuit of pleasure.

I've fucked him enough times to know when he's cresting his own wave, ready to crash over the other side.

I readjust, slipping my hand below the desk so I can stroke myself and release my own torture.

"Fuck, Captain," he groans out. "I'm about to make a mess of you."

"Bloody hell." I find the rhythm I want as Roc pounds into me, his hips ramming against my ass, my hips pounding against the desk.

His thrusts change in cadence and then he's ramming into me, grunting through an orgasm.

I'm so close.

So fucking close.

Roc shoves my head forward, hand like a claw in my hair, the other hand sinking to my balls, squeezing just enough so a lance of pain mixes with the pleasure and sending a shock wave from my gut down into my groin.

The pressure builds, the tingling rocketing up my cock as I come.

A rope of cum shoots out, hitting the cuff of my hand, dribbling onto the floor.

I heave out a breath and a loose paper flutters off my desk and disappears from sight.

Roc presses forward, still breathing hard, and gives my hair a tousle. "Good boy, Captain."

Another jolt rocks through me and some of the tension in my body finally fizzles out.

CHAPTER SIX
WENDY

I wake to the sunlight filtering in through the parted drapes in our bedroom.

There is a warm body behind me, a strong arm curled around my waist. I know immediately that it's Roc. He burns hotter than James and while both men are cut like marble, Roc is just slightly more cut.

"Good morning," I mumble against my feather pillow and stretch out my legs.

Roc's nose grazes the side of my neck, inhaling my scent, before he plants a kiss on my bare shoulder. "Hello, my Darling."

"Is it early?"

"Yes."

"James is already up, isn't he?"

"Yes."

I'm always the last out of bed. I screwed up my circadian rhythm in the Everland Palace, preferring to stay up to the early hours of the morning when no one was around to judge me or bother me except for Asha, whose company I always preferred, regardless of the time of day. So now I am a night creature who sleeps well into mid-morning. Thankfully Roc is also a night creature so some of our rhythm matches up. He just needs fewer hours of sleep than I do so he's usually up before I am.

"I have a request," Roc says, kissing another bare spot on my shoulder.

"What is it?"

"On our wedding night," he pushes into me and while he isn't fully hard, there is definitely thickness to his cock, and it nestles between the globes of my ass. "I'd like it if you took us both."

I tense. He notices.

"Which leads me to today's request."

He slips away from me and stretches across the expanse of our king's bed, grabbing something from his bedside table. When he returns to me, he drapes his arm over me, holding a small object in front of my face.

It's matte black, shaped like a teardrop with a flat disc-like bottom.

"A plug," I say.

"Wear it for me. Day by day. And come our wedding night, you will be ready."

I might not have had much experience with sex as the Queen of Everland, forced into celibacy because of my agreement with Hald, but I still heard all of the courtly gossip that swirled around the palace. Asha wasn't one to sleep and tell, but occasionally she would share a detail or two. So yes, I know what a plug is and where it goes. And I know the primary reason one would use it—to prepare for anal sex.

Just the thought makes my insides tense up and a thrill race up my spine.

I'm sure there will be an adjustment period, getting fucked by them both at the same time, a period where it is mixed with both pleasure and pain. But I'm willing to attempt it.

"Okay," I say.

Roc kisses me again, this time on the soft curve of my neck. "You know how to please me, Wendy Darling."

I think I would do anything he asked. But I'm not going to tell him that, though I suspect he already knows.

"Do you want help?" he asks.

I laugh, a little nervous. "Maybe I do this one alone?"

He climbs from the bed, but bends down and kisses me once more. "There's lubrication in the bedside drawer. Pretend it's me when it fills you up." Then he winks and leaves me alone with the plug.

I STARE AT THE THING FOR SEVERAL LONG MINUTES TRYING TO gauge the plausibility of it fitting. It's not bigger than Roc or James, but it seems huge in my hand. I'm determined though, because Roc asked for it and because I do want to be filled up by both of my men on our wedding night.

The bottle of lubrication is one made by the fae. Roc bought it for all of us and we have a stock of several bottles in the bathroom to last us several years. When I use the dropper to dispense a bead on my fingertips, it's immediately warm, slippery, and wet. It truly is the best lube and while I've never asked, I suspect there's some magic mixed into it to help with discomfort. All the better for this experiment.

Now in our bath, the door shut and locked, I take a deep breath and go for it.

The tapered point of the plug is slick with lube and when I place it at my opening, I immediately tense up.

Maybe I should have asked Roc for help.

But it's like ripping off a bandage where the pain is more tolerable when someone else tears it free.

Too late now.

I try again and push in a half inch. The lube makes it easy and after a deep breath, it's in another half inch, just about to its widest part.

The pain is minimal and I just know when it's Roc or James it will likely hurt far more.

I'm ready for the pain. For years, I felt nothing at all.

Steeling myself for the last of it, I brace and push in all the way. It settles inside of me, filling me up, and my inner walls immediately clench around it, echoing in my pussy.

I straighten, trying to relax the muscles around the plug.

In the mirror over the vanity, I can see some of the embarrassment already painting my cheeks.

But the embarrassment quickly morphs to something erotic, like a dirty secret.

If I go out in public wearing this with James or Roc, I'm not sure I'll survive it.

My clit is already throbbing and I haven't even been touched.

Roc clearly knew what he was doing when he suggested I wear it to breakfast. He knew it would spark a reaction, a raw illicitness that floods my entire body and raises my core temperature.

My face is suddenly shiny in the reflection in the mirror, my cheeks painted bright red.

But I'm nothing if not stubborn.

I'm not turning back now.

Slipping on my house slippers, I make my way down to breakfast to face my men with a plug in my ass.

CHAPTER SEVEN
HOOK

I'VE BEEN UP FOR HOURS AND AM ON MY FIFTH CUP OF COFFEE when Roc finally makes his way downstairs. His white button-up is unbuttoned and hanging open, revealing the tightly packed muscle in his stomach. He hasn't put his belt on yet so his black trousers hang low on his hips and the deep V cut is on full display.

I'm suddenly thirsty for something not in a cup.

"Stop ogling me, Captain," he says and picks up a freshly washed apple from the long sideboard. Water is beaded on the waxy skin, and when he sinks his teeth into it, the water and juice dribble down his chin.

Bloody hell.

When I manage to drag my gaze back up to his eyes, he's smiling at me with teeth and fire.

I scowl at him. "You're doing that on purpose."

"Because you're so easy to bait."

I join him at the sideboard where our breakfast spread is laid out. Every morning, it's full of food. Fresh fruit, fresh-baked raisin bread, hard-boiled eggs, buttered toast, mini tarts, and crispy bacon. It's too much food and we never manage to make a dent in it. Roc ordered the kitchen staff to donate what we don't eat to the orphanages on Bassal Street. The kids must be feasting like kings over there.

"Have you seen Wendy?" I ask.

"Mmm." He swallows a mouthful of apple. "She should be down momentarily." There's a secret glimmering in his eyes.

"What is it?"

"Hmm? What do you mean?"

"I know when you're toying with me."

"Only when I make it obvious."

Grabbing a slice of buttered toast, he sits at the head of the long breakfast table where steam rises up from his morning coffee, poured just moments ago by the kitchen staff. Beside it is a ceramic bowl of salted and roasted peanuts.

Now with the Darkland Dark Shadow, he no longer has to feed his supernatural hunger with peanuts, but I suspect he's addicted to them by now, because he's yet to give them up.

With a grumble, I decide it's best to ignore him, because entertaining him only fuels his ego.

Plate in hand, I fill it with bacon, toast, and an egg. I much prefer duck eggs, but the kitchen staff was vehemently against it, insisting the household of a future king must serve eggs from the royal roost and not some backwater animal. But duck eggs contain more protein than chicken eggs, which means they are far superior. But who am I to question the divine qualities of the royal roost?

I don't know if I'll ever get used to living in a regal household. Roc seems to have found his place in it with very little effort. Though I suppose he *was* born into it. He might have never expected to inherit the throne, but he was always part of the royal line, even after his father's actions had their titles stripped.

The full breadth of Roc's life ruling the Umbrage is still largely unknown to me, but because I know *him*, I suspect he acted like a king there, too.

And Wendy, having lived as a queen for half her life, seems to feel right at home. She knows how to speak to the staff with authority, but with respect. She knows how to ask for what she wants without worrying about how she will be perceived.

I'm the only outlier. The only one of us who has spent most of his life fighting for scraps amongst pirates and thieves.

The staff of the house conduct themselves with decorum when they're around us, but it's easy to let my mind conjure backroom whispers where they're discussing my rough edges, my lack of etiquette (which bloody spoon do I use?), and my inability to just fucking relax in luxury.

"Captain."

My gaze snaps up to Roc. Despite the tall, rigid back of our breakfast room dining chairs, he's languid, stretched out like our fucking cat in the sun.

"What?" I ask when he doesn't immediately speak.

He nods at my hand, now a fist on the table. And in my fist is the crushed chicken egg.

"Bloody hell." I toss the egg onto one of the many empty plates on the table. Why are there so many empty plates? The egg is ruined now, with shards of shell wedged into the hard-boiled white.

"There she is," Roc says.

I glance at the arched doorway to find Wendy in a slant of sunlight. She's gorgeous as always, like a divine temple statue come to life.

Her dark hair spills over her shoulders in waves. There is a hint of color on her cheeks, and a frenzied energy in her body, like she ran all the way here.

A day dress tailored just for her skims her hips and pools on the floor around her feet.

"Good morning, love."

She comes over to me and circles me from behind, bending forward to plant a kiss on my cheek.

"You're tense," she says.

"You should have seen his face a moment ago," Roc says.

"What about your face?" she asks me.

"My face was fine."

Roc pops a shelled peanut into his mouth. "Tell that to the egg."

I'm not going to admit to them that I feel like an impostor, like a common thief who picked the lock to smuggle his way in.

"I'm fine," I say and squeeze Wendy's hand. "Truly."

I can feel Roc's gaze on me. He knows I'm lying. But this is mine to bear. I don't need him pitying the poor pirate who has now found himself in the lap of luxury, fucking a king and queen.

I just...I need time to adjust.

I will.

Eventually.

Probably.

Sensing Wendy's arrival, the faremaid enters the room with the sterling silver coffee carafe and fills Wendy's mug. Wendy goes to the sideboard and fills a plate with bread and fruit.

She takes the chair across from me, but squirms on the seat.

"Is something wrong?" I ask her. "Is it the chair? Roc, I told you the chairs in here are abhorrently uncomfortable."

Roc chuckles to himself and cracks open another peanut.

Wendy's face turns bright red.

"What?" I ask, clearly having missed something.

Wendy adds a splash of cream to her coffee and twirls the spoon around, waiting for the faremaid to leave the room.

Once we're alone, Wendy leans in and lowers her voice. "There's a...plug...in..." She swallows. Roc tosses back another peanut. "I'm wearing a plug," she says quickly.

"What? What the bloody hell for?" I shift to Roc. "Is this your idea?"

The amusement slips from his face. "Yes. I don't want to take turns anymore. She'll take us both and this is the best way to prepare her."

"She doesn't have to. Wendy, love, you don't have to."

"I want to."

"But..."

"Captain." Roc has abandoned the peanuts and is now sitting straight up, the line of his shoulders straight and rigid. "What are you worried about?"

Wendy shifts again on the edge of her seat.

"She's clearly uncomfortable."

"Yes, Captain. Because there is a plug in her ass."

Wendy nearly spits out her mouthful of coffee.

"She shouldn't endure for us. She doesn't have to pretend to be a whore to appease you or I."

The room goes silent and my voice seems to ring out all around us like a ripple in water.

"James," Wendy starts but Roc cuts her off.

"No, Darling." Roc pushes away from the table. "Don't

save him. Let him sit with that." He goes over to Wendy and offers his hand. "I'd like you to accompany me to the high chamber today."

"Me? For what purpose?"

"We're discussing charity work today."

It's immediately apparent in the way Wendy perks up that this interests her more than breakfast.

Taking Roc's hand, she stands. "Let me change."

"I'll have the staff pack your breakfast."

She nods and glances quickly at me, but I can't face her now, can I?

When she's gone, Roc stands there behind her empty chair for a beat. The quiet is disconcerting. Now that Roc has claimed the Darkland Dark Shadow, his presence in any room is different than it was before. Like sharing space with a black hole. You are at once in awe of the raw power and terrified of disappearing inside of it.

The hair lifts on the back of my neck.

I can't seem to look at him. I can't seem to do anything other than sit here in my chair like a wounded animal.

"Why are you coddling her?" he finally says.

I know the answer.

It's trembling on the back of my tongue. Churning in the pit of my stomach.

Roc has always existed in both of these worlds—royal elegance and filthy, dark depravity.

And every day of my life, I've tried to push down my darker urges. The entire time I hunted Peter Pan, I told myself it was for the greater good when deep down I knew there was more to it than that. I just wanted to best him. I wanted to wrap my hands around his throat and watch the life drain out of him, the great, indomitable Peter Pan.

And I'm worried if I continue to give in to my dark side

here, everyone will know that the pirate Captain James Hook doesn't belong. And I would never want that for Wendy.

Bloody hell.

"I want to be good for her," I finally say, my voice barely above a whisper. "And you."

He comes around the table and puts a hand on my shoulder. He just stands there for a handful of heartbeats. We say nothing and everything.

Then, "Do you think she needs you to be good?" He doesn't wait for my answer. "Your need for perfection will eventually eat you from the inside, Captain. Until there's nothing left."

He runs his fingers through my hair in a way that is both endearing and admonishing and then leaves me to fester in my own gloom.

Dear Smee,
I'm getting married. Can you believe it?

I would be greatly honored if you attended as my witness.

But beyond that, I miss you, Smee.
I miss you terribly.

-Jas

CHAPTER EIGHT
WENDY

I'VE BEEN TO THE HIGH CHAMBER TWICE BEFORE TODAY BUT BOTH times I was visiting Roc with James by my side and it was never under official business.

Today I'm to act in the capacity of the future Queen of Darkland.

It is both familiar and foreign. Familiar because I know what it is to be queen to a powerful man. Foreign because this time around, I have chosen the role instead of being forced into it.

The stakes are much higher. Which is absolutely wild considering in Everland, my life was always on the line.

Now it's not my life on the line, but Roc's reputation, and mine.

Ruling Darkland is our future and I want it to be done well and right.

But James's words at breakfast are running through my mind and I can't seem to focus.

I almost feel bad for him. He was clearly trying to protect me, but he went about it all wrong, robbing me of my free will to decide what I want and how I want it. I don't need his protection.

Our carriage pulls through the gate at the back of the High Chamber building.

There's a row of guards stationed along the winding cobblestone drive, all of them dressed in Darkland black.

I turn to Roc who sits beside me on the leather bench seat. His gaze is trained out the window, his fingers pressed against his full lips. He's been deep in thought since we left Maddred Manor.

"Roc."

"Hmm?"

"What's going on with James? Has he said anything to you? Do you think he's bothered by you proposing to me first?"

He turns to me. I try not to squirm beneath his gaze, but the plug makes it doubly hard to sit still.

"Our Captain is having a hard time adjusting, I suspect, and he's just looking for things to handle."

"I thought he was fitting in at the Portage Hall?"

"The minister is trying to undermine him."

Oh. I didn't know. James hasn't said anything about it. But in any case... "Isn't the minister the one in charge?"

"Yes. *For now.*"

I don't get the chance to ask him what that means because the carriage comes to a halting stop and the door is pulled open by one of the attendants at the king's private entrance.

Roc's assistant, Tyrin, is immediately by his side, rattling off a list of priorities.

Tyrin is in his late twenties with a shock of black hair and gold-framed round spectacles that he occasionally has to push back on the bridge of his nose. There's a gold stud in his left ear to match the glasses and a gold chain around his neck. Whatever hangs on the end is always hidden beneath his clothing, but from the outline of the pendant, I'd guess it was a skull and crossbones—the symbol of the Bone Society.

I haven't asked yet if Tyrin is a Jabberwocky or a functionary member of the secret society that Roc's family founded.

Tyrin does keep a close eye on the time, but he's the assistant to the future king of Darkland. If he doesn't keep time, who will?

"Your meeting with the Council was scheduled to begin ten minutes ago," Tyrin says. "But I've held them in chamber waiting for your arrival."

"Is the daquis here?"

"Yes, she's in the outer chamber with Councilmember Gorson until we're ready for her."

"Lovely."

The daquis is the head of all the orphanages in Darkland. From what I've been told, she's been in charge for over a decade and, unlike her predecessor, has actually made a difference. But Darkland is still short on beds. Building space for orphans was one of my tasks in Everland, but I was constantly fighting Hally, the Crowned Prince, for funding. He saw no use for it. "Put them to work on the farms so they can learn the lesson of hard work," he'd told me one day. "Children work faster anyway."

I wanted to punch him in his dumb fucking face after he said that, but because I was always running from something in Everland, I tended to keep my mouth shut and not rock the boat.

Quietly, with the help of a few sympathetic baronesses, we were able to pool some funding together and build a modest twenty-five-bed orphanage on the outskirts of South Avis, the capital of Everland, in a place Hally would never bother to fuss over.

It's still one of the things I'm most proud of having built while wearing the Everland crown.

To have the chance to use that experience here on Darkland would be an absolute joy. Not only because I learned a lot the first time around, but because I won't have to fight a spoiled prince for funding. Roc will give me whatever I ask for. I'm sure of it. Those kids are getting fleece blankets and feather pillows if I have any say about it.

The building that houses the High Chamber's offices is situated in the center of Wicking Hill. The Hill is where all of Darkland's important offices and functionaries are located, in a long, narrow strip of land that runs north and south.

While I love all of Darkland's architecture (it's certainly more ornate and beautiful than Everland's plain stone and timber), I think the High Chamber building is my favorite. The front facade features four huge marble columns that hold up a pediment with relief carvings of snakes intertwined in human skeletons.

Snakes and skulls, as Asha informed me, are important symbols in Darkland history and culture, so they continue throughout all of the administrative buildings with skulls carved into the doorknobs and snakes featured in several stained-glass transom windows over the interior doorways.

As Roc makes his way across the main gallery to the council chamber, people slowly gravitate toward him.

There are other lower-level members of his council, several pages with urgent letters, a few onlookers who just want to be near him, and a handful of Darklanders hoping for an audience.

I understand that draw better than anyone.

I hang back, letting him take center stage.

Even as Queen of Everland, I tended to slink into the shadows, out of the spotlight. I don't like people looking at me too closely.

When we reach the other side of the gallery, Roc pauses and turns around.

The crowd he's accumulated stops with him.

"Wendy, Darling," he calls and holds out his hand for me.

The crowd pulls back, giving me room.

I swallow, suddenly feeling like it must be obvious I'm wearing a plug even though there's no way anyone could possibly know.

I step forward into the center of the crowd and Roc takes my hand. He bends down and puts his mouth to my ear, whispering so only I can hear. "As my future queen, you are to be by my side, hmm?"

My body fills with heat at the promise of what's to come, and the thread of authority that rings out in his voice.

"Of course."

We start walking again. The crowd picks up, matching our pace as we leave the gallery behind.

INSIDE THE HIGH CHAMBER, I'M GIVEN THE CHAIR ON ROC'S LEFT, signifying a position of importance. No one argues.

His council is comprised of seven members, four of them being women. In Everland, the entire council was made up of white men, and half of them got their positions because they had been born to the right family or inherited the right amount of money.

When I mentioned looking further outside of his personal circle for councilmembers to help diversify, King Hald told me he would consider my concerns and bring them up at the next council meeting. But it never changed. In fact, it only got worse once Hald slipped into a coma and Hally took over.

Two members of Roc's council were grandfathered in from the previous council—the Portage Minister, Yal Mertz, and Isle Minister, Sun Yun. The rest were appointed personally by Roc—Minister of the Interior, Ulonda Uzo; Merchant Minister, Kahl Evvie II; Agriculture Minister, Penny Sorren; Minister of War, Rebba Rohl; and Treasure Minister, Gregor Anson.

I haven't worked with them in any official capacity, but if I had to guess, based on how Roc speaks about them and having read up on some of their work, Ulonda is the smartest, Rebba is the most badass, and Kahl worked his way up from nothing.

I can't imagine a better council.

Roc could continue his life of luxury and leisure and hand over the hard work of running a country to anyone who wanted the power and the prestige, but seeing the council he's put together, I know he means to do it right.

The meeting is opened with a few line items about an upcoming parade, the coronation, and repairs to the Treasury Building.

The daquis is brought into the meeting after that and the council discusses possible land to build not one, but two buildings for children in need. Because the interior is under Ulonda's purview, we make plans for later on to tour a few possible locations, though the entire council is in agreement that the land located in the rolling hills to the west of the city would be the best.

The daquis takes down my contact information and promises to schedule a personal meeting with me soon.

After the daquis leaves, Yal Mertz pivots to portage.

"We've been having trouble again with the Gutter Snakes importing stolen goods. A ship slipped through three nights ago and I anticipate another tomorrow night."

"That's unfortunate." Roc lights a cigarette and leans back in his chair. "How much are they paying you?"

Yal's face goes red. "I beg your pardon!"

"Your Grace."

"What?"

"It's, 'I beg your pardon, Your Grace,'" Roc corrects.

Yal pushes his chair back. "If they were paying me, would I have brought it up to you?"

"Yes." Roc takes a hit and when the smoke comes back out, it curls up to his nose where he sucks it back in. "Because, and correct me if I'm wrong, you heard I have a spy in the Gutter Snakes so you thought you'd get ahead of it."

Yal's nostrils flare. "Just tell me what you'd like me to do, *Your Grace*."

"Deny them port of entry."

"They'll retaliate."

"They're the fucking Gutter Snakes, Mertz. They are the least sophisticated gang in all of the Umbrage."

"Very well." Yal takes a breath. "If that's all?"

"Not quite." Roc takes another pull on his cigarette. "When do you leave for the next export?"

"I...you—"

"I'll tell you," Roc says. "Tonight. Sail thee well, Mertz."

The Portage Minister shoves his chair into the table and storms from the room.

"That will come back to bite you," Ulonda says.

"Nah." Roc stubs out his cigarette in a nearby tray. "He'll be dead within a week."

If anyone is shocked by this, they don't betray it.

The council wraps up a few additional items before dispersing.

When we're alone, Roc turns to me. "I liked having you by my side."

I snort. "Don't lie to me."

"I'm not."

"I barely spoke."

"But when you did, it was with authority."

"I—"

"Take the admiration, Wendy," he orders.

"Okay. Thank you."

He gets up and comes around to kiss me on the cheek. "You will be a radiant queen. Darkland won't know what to do with you."

I lean into him as his fingers trail from my jawline down my throat. "What about James?"

"I have plans for him too. If he'll stop fighting me."

I huff out a laugh. "I doubt he ever will."

"He will if he knows what's good for him."

Roc steps away and I jolt to the side, immediately feeling his absence. He goes to the three arched windows at the front of the chamber room that overlook the boulevard that spills into the High Chamber gardens. With his back to me, he says, "You don't have to be our whore if you don't want to be."

I leave the table and come up behind him, wrapping my

arms around his waist. His stomach is firm beneath my clasped hands, his abs rippled like the cobblestones below.

I won't tell him I'd do anything for him. He doesn't want a sycophant. If I kowtow to him then I am just like everyone else in his orbit.

"I spent the better half of my life pretending to be a good girl. I don't want to pretend any longer."

He glances at me over his shoulder, the corner of his mouth lifting. "Don't tempt me, Wendy Darling. I will have you sinning for me by moonrise."

I laugh. "Perhaps *you* are tempting *me*."

He hooks his arm around me, coaxing me forward into his side. I love being in his embrace. The thrill of standing beside him has yet to wear off and I hope it never does.

"I guess I just have to reassure James that I want to be corrupted."

Roc chuckles and twirls his finger in my hair. "If we team up, I'm sure we can convince him."

I nod into him. "We're clever enough to come up with some ideas."

He tightens his grip, taking a handful of my hair and yanking my head back, exposing my throat. He leaves a trail of kisses up and up before coming to my mouth. "I will look forward to it."

CHAPTER NINE
WENDY

We spend the next two weeks planning for the wedding and the coronation that will follow a few days after.

This may be my second wedding, but the first time around, my marriage to King Hald was entirely out of my control. The flowers were selected to match the Everland colors. The linens were the same linens used for every royal wedding dating back a hundred years. Even the music was pre-selected.

Now, I can literally have anything, and I'm finding it paralyzing.

Thankfully, I managed to steal Asha away from the Darkland Archives to join me and James today.

In the months we've been on Darkland, Asha has easily slipped back into her old role within the Archives, but this time she's very close to the top, now in the role of Executive Archivist. I've barely seen her since we settled in on the island and not for lack of trying.

I've sent her a messenger every single day, sometimes with chocolate or silk scarf attached.

Her last reply was, "Are you trying to buy my affection?"

To which I replied YES, spelled out in white roses in a gilded box hand-carved by woodworking artisans from the northern coast.

I think it was the roses that finally convinced her I need her like I need air.

Asha riffles through a stack of napkins and pulls out a black linen square with snakes embroidered in silver along the bottom. "This is very Darkland."

"Let's go with that one," James says.

"You said that about the last one," I point out. "And it was blue."

"I like blue."

"We are not a blue-wedding type of people."

"Aren't we?"

"No."

He scowls at me. He's been in a foul mood lately and I can't tell if it's me, Roc, the wedding, or something else. We never did return to the whore comment he made at breakfast a few weeks ago. I let him pretend he never said it and he seems fine with pretending he didn't.

But it's been hanging in the air between us.

I take the napkin from Asha and rub the material between my fingers. "It's kinda rough, don't you think?"

Mr. Lo, the textile expert, a middle-aged man with salt and pepper hair and a neatly trimmed mustache, nods his agreement. "This particular linen is made of the flax plants that are harvested in the midlands of Winterland. It has a very specific, rustic look and if I could recommend something that would match the atmosphere of a king's wedding..."

"Yes, of course," I coax.

"Ms. Taira has the right idea," he says, nodding at Asha.

"As the future queen of Darkland, black would serve you best. And the snakes are iconic, as you know. But we have this softer cotton blend." He retrieves another sample from a rack behind him.

The design is almost an exact replica of the first, but the cotton is definitely softer than the linen when rubbed between my fingers.

"Let's go with that one," I say before I get confused by other options.

"Finally," James mutters.

"Excellent choice," Mr. Lo says. "How many will you need?"

I glance at Asha, then James. "What did we settle on? Five hundred?"

"I don't know why you're asking me," Asha says with a laugh. "I didn't write the guest list."

"Five hundred. I think."

"Very well. I'll get the order written up. Where should we deliver them?"

"The wedding is taking place at the Dark Cathedral," James says. "With the reception following right after in the adjoining Banquet Hall. If you could please deliver them there, that would be preferred."

"Of course. It would be my pleasure. And if anything changes, please let me know." Mr. Lo gives us a quick nod and then returns to his work behind the counter.

James, Asha and I leave the textile shop and exit onto the thoroughfare that runs between a row of shops in the Merchant District. Paper lanterns are strung overhead, zigzagging back and forth across the fareway with a row of cafe tables beneath. Several of the tables are full with couples and friend groups chatting over pastries and coffee.

"How come we never come here for an afternoon?" I ask.

Asha breaks away to buy a bag of *piril* candies from a cart vendor.

"It's a security risk," James answers as we pause to wait for Asha. "I'm shocked Roc let you come today without an escort."

I roll my eyes at him. "I have you and Asha. Besides, if you think I don't know that Hagan is trailing me at all times, then you don't think very highly of me."

He sighs. "Well I haven't confirmed that she is. I've yet to spot her. Have you?"

"No. But I know she's there."

Asha returns, opening the white paper bag of candies with a sharp tear. "Who is where?"

"Hagan," I tell her.

"Oh yeah. She is very good at what she does." Asha pulls out a candy, this one shaped like a star with white sprinkles rolled into the chocolate coating. "Do you know where she trained?"

We keep walking and pass a group of twenty-some-things and they all watch us, then whisper to each other.

The stretch of time when I could be on Darkland soil and remain anonymous was short-lived.

Before too long, Roc will insist I have more than just Hagan and it will be obvious who I am wherever I go.

"Roc didn't say," James answers.

I steal a candy from Asha's bag. Mine is round and coated in red chocolate. "It can't be basic training."

Asha squints into the sunlight as we exit the fareway and hit the sidewalk on the next street. "I agree. She's highly skilled and her ability to blend into her surroundings is a talent I don't see very often. Especially for someone of her size."

I break open the candy between my back teeth. "You have that look."

"Well…" Asha pops another candy in her mouth. "It's a theory."

"Yes, I know. That's your I-have-a-theory look."

She laughs. "I think your Hagan is from Wonderland."

I make a face at James, all wide-eyed and mouth agape. "Did you know that?"

"No. Roc doesn't tell me anything about his past but I suppose the theory makes sense—"

"Captain Hook!"

A young man with dark, wavy hair and light brown skin comes barreling down the sidewalk. He's wearing one of the navy blue overcoats that tells me he's within the portage office, and the three stripes sewn into his sleeve signify his rank as a communication officer, if I remember correctly.

James once spent an afternoon telling me all about rankings and patches and uniform pins within the portage office. That man loves a hierarchy, even better if the rules within the hierarchy are explicitly laid out. I think the rules are like a balm to his mind.

"Manuel? What is it?" James asks.

"We just received word about Mertz's ship."

James's face falls. "Is it bad?"

Manuel frowns. "You should come to the hall for the debriefing."

James nods and then leans into me, kissing my forehead. "I'll meet you at home later."

"Is everything all right?" I ask. Yal Mertz is the Portage

Minister. I don't think they're friends, but maybe I missed that detail.

"It will be," James tells me. "Asha, will you make sure she reaches home safely?"

"Of course."

James and Manuel are off running before Asha finishes her sentence.

CHAPTER TEN
HOOK

When Manuel and I enter the Portage Hall, Roc is already there.

A ribbon of smoke snakes from the end of his lit cigarette. He's sitting at one of the porter desks, the chair rocked back, his boots crossed and propped on the edge of the desk.

"Finally," he says, his head lulled back, his eyes on me.

I shiver despite the heat in the room.

It's been hot these last few days with barely any wind and no rain in sight.

The worst possible conditions for a shipping route through the sirens' mating territory. Heat agitates them and with a lack of wind, ships are at their mercy.

"Why are you here?" I ask Roc, trying not to sound accusatory. After all, he's the interim leader of Darkland and soon-to-be official leader. He can go where he pleases.

"Are you not happy to see me, Captain?" The chair thuds forward when his boots drop from the desk. Ash falls from his cigarette onto the marble floor.

"That's beside the point," I say with a grumble.

He winks at me and takes a long hit from his cigarette. When he exhales smoke, he says, "I heard the awful news about Yal's ship and came at once."

I'll just bet he did.

"What's the word?" I ask the crew.

There are several pages, along with Manuel, and two young men from the telegrapher's office as indicated by the circular patch on their uniforms.

The shorter of the two men steps forward and removes his hat, breaking the brim in his anxious hands. "We got word just an hour ago that Yal Mertz's ship went down taking the entire crew with it."

"I hate to say 'I told you so...'" Roc says. "Well...Mertz isn't here anyway, so I guess that is moot."

"Roc." I shoot him a chastising look, but he just rolls his eyes.

"We did warn him, Captain."

"*I* warned him."

"So you did."

"And you sent him off anyway."

Roc waves me away. "That's what he gets for being a massive prick."

The entire room has gone silent, watching this exchange. I'm the newcomer here. An outlier. The boyfriend of the future king. I barely hold weight. And yet, there is the sensation of held breath, as if they are all waiting for me to say something.

"We lower the flags to half mast," I order.

"Right away," one of the pages says, a young woman with dark hair pinned up in a bun. She scurries off.

"Send someone to Mertz's house to inform his wife."

"I'm on it," another page says and disappears through the nearest exit.

"Let's cross-check the cargo list on Mertz's ship," I go on. "And make sure we have adequate insurance to replace what the merchants lost."

"Landee and I will work on that," Manuel says, nodding at the young woman with the desk beside his.

"Looks like we have a new portage minister," Roc says.

I come to a stop. "That's not—*no*. It should go to—"

Manuel interrupts me. "Beg your pardon, Your Grace. But can you have the council assembled tonight? If so, I can draft the articles of induction so he can be sworn in immediately."

"Yes," Roc answers and smiles at me.

"Absolutely not! There is a hierarchy here and it must be adhered to and—"

"Yes," Manuel says, his silver pen in hand. "There is a hierarchy, and the future king of Darkland has made a demand. We are meant to follow it."

I glance at Roc, now leaning against the desk, arms crossed over his chest, his spent cigarette still smoldering in the nearby crystal ashtray. His smile widens, all teeth.

I don't bother asking him if this was his plan all along.

I already know the answer.

WITHIN A FEW HOURS, I'M IN THE HIGH CHAMBER WITH ROC AND his council members. In order to be inducted onto the council, we need a majority approval first. That means four yays.

Roc stands at the head of the room, slightly hunched, his hands on the table, veins swirling over his knuckles. His jacket is off, shirtsleeves rolled up to his elbows, revealing all of the ink on his skin.

Looking at him, one would not automatically see a king. But I think that's exactly why he makes such an impressive one, or soon-to-be. He doesn't fit the mold.

In a chair on his left, I have a clear view of the entire council and despite the late hour, they are all put together, like they belong here, like they were born to lead a country.

I don't really know any of these people, not personally.

I've avoided the council and the high chamber up until this point, telling myself that Roc and I were too busy for such frivolity. But sitting here now at the long, rectangular chamber table topped in gleaming marble, I realize that was an excuse to avoid feeling like an impostor.

I shift on the edge of my chair. The movement causes my hook to hit the marble and the metal lets out a loud ting.

Several councilmembers glance at me.

I just want this to be over.

This is a bad fucking idea.

I should just get up right now and tell Roc he needs to find someone else.

"Thank you all for reporting on such short notice." Roc straightens and crosses his arms over his chest. All of the muscles in his forearms twine and dance. "We just learned Mertz's ship went down. As you can imagine, I don't want to leave his seat open for too long. Imports and exports are some of our most important assets."

"But do you think it's such a good idea to be nominating your boyfriend?"

That from a man down the table. I think that's Kahl Evvie II, the merchant minister. I suppose he, more than anyone, should have an opinion on who the portage minister is, since much of what he oversees comes in through the harbor.

"Do you know who warned Mertz about the siren mating territories? The one who urged him to shift the shipping lanes?" Roc asks the council.

Of course they don't know. They all remain silent.

"Captain James Hook," Roc tells them.

I can feel them reassessing me.

"He has more experience on the seas than half the Seven Isles. He knows every season, every sea creature. He may be my boyfriend, but there is no one more qualified."

Am I blushing? I am blushing.

I do not take compliments well and praise is even harder. Especially professional praise.

I'm a pirate. Not a businessman.

And yet my back straightens and my shoulders level out as if Roc's words have filled my spine with steel.

"Very well," one of the councilmembers says.

"I have no objections," the woman down on the left says.

"To a vote," Roc says. "All those in favor of Captain James Hook being inducted to the High Chamber as Portage Minister, say aye."

All seven councilmembers say, "Aye," in unison.

And so it is done.

CHAPTER ELEVEN
HOOK

As much as I want to resist Roc and his plans, I do settle into my role as Portage Minister quite well.

I do know the seas of the Seven Isles better than most, and plotting routes, checking for risk and efficiency soothes my brain.

I suspect Roc knew how much I would love this role, but I don't love how he went about acquiring it for me.

An entire crew is gone.

Though Mertz's pride helped fulfill that prophecy.

If he had just listened to me...

Manuel becomes my right-hand quickly. Like me, he enjoys order. At the end of the day, his desk is arranged, papers stacked, pens set in their case. He is very good at spotting potential risks and adjusting as necessary. Unlike Mertz, he doesn't allow himself to get hung up on whether he's right or wrong. If there is a better way, then he embraces it and moves on.

I fall into a rhythm that helps calm some of my nerves about the upcoming wedding. Most mornings, I have breakfast with Wendy and Roc. Roc leaves first because he is always needed somewhere urgently.

Wendy will dismiss herself from the breakfast table to get ready and I usually find myself in the library with a cigarello and Firecracker. The cat is a menace, but I am loath to move him when he finds a comfortable spot on my lap and curls into a perfect ball.

Once Wendy is done, we walk together to the clinic, where I kiss her goodbye and then continue on to the Portage Hall.

But on the seventh day of this new routine, I come to a sudden halt when a familiar face catches my eye.

I blink several times against the sharp slant of sunlight as if my eyes may be deceiving me.

Please be real.

A carriage clatters past and the man shouts at me to move, but I'm already running.

I race up the stairs to the wide veranda outside the Portage Hall and practically lunge at Smee.

My arms are around her and I'm smashing her into me before good manners and good sense flood in.

She smells like home. Like rum and sweet tobacco and fresh Neverland air.

My eyes are burning and my chin wobbling and I can't lose my wits out here where everyone can see, but I am very close to it.

Poor form. *Poor form.*

"Jas," she says.

"Smee." I breathe out, blink rapidly, trying to get control of myself. "You got my letter."

She chuckles beneath me, squeezes me back. "Man of few words. But all the right ones."

I finally disentangle myself from her. Her locs are held

back by a scarf the color of deep rust. She's wearing her usual white button-up blouse and vest, but this vest is black with no adornment. Several delicate gold chains hang around her neck. There's a sparrow pendant, an acorn, and a stamped medallion. Dark, rectangular lenses are over her eyes, shielding from the sunlight. It's a new fashion accessory I can't quite seem to embrace, but Smee makes the glasses look good.

"I...*you*...I wasn't sure you'd come."

"You're getting married," she answers. "Of course I'd come."

"The way we left things..."

"We will always find our way back to one another, Jas. For better or for worse."

"To the edge of the world?"

It's an old saying of ours, back when we spent most of our days on the sea. It was an oath we swore to one another when pirating was even more cutthroat and magic and myth were as dangerous as the monsters that haunted the sea.

"To the edge of the world," she answers.

I clasp my hands behind me and nod, the burn still affecting my eyes. Now I wish I had a pair of dark glasses to hide the watery gleam.

I clear my throat, suck in a breath. I will not cry here on the street in the morning sun.

"I was just about to start my day of work, but I could hold off for a bit if you'd like to get coffee?"

Smee nods. "I'd like that."

There are several cafes around the halls and High Chamber, but I take Smee to my favorite one, a bit of a hole in the wall, because it's usually quieter and lately, my presence in the busier cafes has been noticed.

"Morning, Captain Hook!" the cafe's owner calls out when we enter, the bell above the door chiming.

"Good morning, Tellaro. I brought a friend in today to show off your tasty croissants and your coffee."

Tellaro is one of the winged fae, formerly of Neverland. He moved here after the last fae king was assassinated, at first working in the Umbrage, before moving further uptown to open his own cafe. I like his place because his coffees are straightforward, his pastries perfectly crafted.

As he moves behind the counter, his bright red wings gleam beneath the light—a stark contrast from his tawny skin and long black hair.

Tellaro hands off a mug to his last customer before turning to me and Smee. "Welcome in, friend of Captain Hook. Hopefully, what we have on offer is to your liking."

"Smee," Smee says and gives him a nod. "Jas usually knows the best coffee around, so I'm sure it will be good."

Tellaro smiles as he dries his hand on a towel. "Do you like chocolate? I just pulled out a batch of chocolate croissants. But I also have plain, the Captain's favorite. Or raisin if you're mad as a hatter."

"Chocolate would be great," Smee says. "And black coffee."

"My usual," I tell the fae.

"Coming right up."

Smee and I take one of the round cafe tables near the front window. I don't like crowds inside, but I do enjoy watching them when they're on the outside.

Sometimes when I sit here alone I can't help but watch

the people passing by, wondering if they also suffer from crippling impostor syndrome, or the fear that they will never be enough.

"So tell me anything and everything. Tell me what you've been up to," I say.

I'm eager to hear about her new life as a pirate captain and just as eager to hear if Neverland has changed.

"Peter Pan and the Lost Boys have been behaving themselves," she says and leans back into her chair. "Winnie Darling has changed them to a degree that is almost hard to recognize. We've struck an alliance, one that I think is fair to all of us, and we no longer have territory lines. They can come and go as they please, and the same goes for our side."

My mouth is hanging open. I only realize it when Smee stops and frowns at me.

"There is a truce?" I ask.

She nods, and the pride in her work is clear on her face.

"You've done what I could never do, Smee." I swallow again, feeling that now familiar swell of emotion. "Well done."

She waves me off. "Clearly, the problem was you. Once you were gone, we were all good friends."

I snort.

She laughs.

"But in all honesty, Neverland feels like it's been repaired and I'm not going to take that for granted."

Tellaro comes over with our coffees first. His mugs are white with a stamp of red wings on each side. Steam rises up, perfuming the air with fresh roasted coffee that's a little nutty, and very rich.

"Croissants are on their way out," he says and returns to the counter for the next customer.

"What about your crew? Have you had luck there?"

Mug in hand, she blows across it, sending the steam swirling. "I've found a few good men. And women."

"Oh?"

We were always an equal opportunity crew, but women were harder to recruit for various reasons, despite our efforts.

"All in all, it's going well." She sips from the coffee and widens her eyes. "Oh, this is good."

"See!"

I taste from mine, delighting in the richness of it, and the joy of sharing it with my closest friend.

"What about Cherry?" I ask. "Were you able to get her somewhere safe?"

I last left my little sister on board my destroyed ship when Roc, Wendy, Vane, Winnie, and Asha, and I sailed for Darkland. All of it happened so fast—Roc losing control of his monster, Vane and Winnie joining us—that I barely had time to send a message off to Smee before we left.

"I did," Smee answers now, but there is an uprise in her tone of voice that tells me there is far more to that answer than she is saying.

"But?" I coax. "Did she give you trouble? Did she try to throw herself at a Lost Boy again?"

"Jas," Smee chides.

"Well." I huff.

I can predict the movements of a storm surge much better than I can predict my little sister. And some of that is my fault.

I traded her for Smee many years ago in my endless war with Peter Pan. It's a decision I will never forgive myself for. I was blinded by ambition and self-righteousness.

"So where is she?" I ask.

Smee sets her mug down. "She made a choice."

Now I'm on edge. "Smee."

"She's a grown woman, Jas."

"Where is she?"

"She was recruited by the Ancient Order of Shadows."

"What!"

"Jas!"

I exhale and resettle and inhale deeply.

The Ancient Order of Shadows is a not-so-secret society that trains assassins. My little sister is not cut out for that life.

"Why the hell would they recruit her?"

"Maybe because they saw potential in her?"

Smee's words bear a fruit of accusation. One that implies I do not see potential in Cherry. I will admit that I've expected very little of her over the course of our lives. And perhaps some of that led to her constantly seeking approval and admiration from Vane, one of Peter Pan's Lost Boys and Roc's little brother.

That also did not end well.

"Who recruited her?"

"Nix," Smee answers and the absolute dread that follows the sound of that name makes me turn to ice.

"Bloody hell." I hang my head.

"Nix is *the* Shadow. There is no higher authority in the Order. If he saw something in Cherry, let her prove herself and see where it takes her."

"She'll be dead in a day."

"Or maybe she'll make something of herself."

I look across the table at her. "You really think so?"

"You're about to marry the Crocodile. If you ask me, Jas, anything is possible these days."

I rock back into my chair. This conversation is

reminding me, painfully, of the comment I made at breakfast a while back, aimed at Wendy and what I assumed, wrongly, she was doing to please Roc and me.

At the time, I thought I was protecting her, but I think my own fears were getting in the way. Just like they are now with my little sister.

I owe Wendy an apology. And soon.

"Smee, you always were the wisest of us."

She smiles at me. "I know that, Jas. But feel free to continue to remind us whenever the mood strikes."

I SPEND MOST OF THE DAY WITH SMEE SHOWING HER AROUND THE Merchant District. We part ways in the afternoon so she can return to her hotel to rest after her voyage.

I leave the Portage Hall early and head straight to the clinic. I find Wendy reading a storybook to a child sick with pneumonia. When she's finished and the evening nurse arrives to take the child's vitals, Wendy spots me waiting in the hall.

"James," she starts but I cut her off.

"I need to talk to you."

She frowns. "Okay."

There's a courtyard in this wing of the clinic, with a gurgling stone fountain at its center, surrounded by a ring of stone benches and right now the courtyard is empty.

I usher Wendy through the arched doorway and to the closest bench.

"I need to apologize to you."

"James—"

"No. Let me get this out." I take a deep breath. "That comment I made…" I lower my voice even though we're alone. "About the plug. I shouldn't have said that. It's your choice to do as you please. I was...projecting onto you and it was poor form. My entire life, I've been trying to live up to the perceived expectations of my father and I suppose it's been harder to let go of those expectations than I first realized. And being here with you and Roc, and what it all means to be with him, *a king*, and you, a queen, I think it triggered some of those old feelings. But it wasn't fair that I take it out on you and for that I apologize."

She reaches over and takes my hand, bringing it to her lap. "Apology accepted."

I feel the line of my brow sink. "Just like that?"

"Yes, James. Just like that."

"But—"

She leans over and kisses me on the cheek. "Thank you for apologizing. But truthfully, I would have forgiven you with or without it. I know you're still healing from your past. I think we all are. And there are bound to be more conflicts in the future because of it. What matters is that we work through those things together. Don't keep it bottled up. Yeah?"

Relief washes through me. "Yes."

She pats my cheek. "Good. Now be a gentleman and walk me home. I'm tired and this is the last night we have before our Wedding Eve and we have so much more to prepare for."

She's up and headed toward the door before I can say another word.

The thought crosses my mind that I don't deserve her, how kind and caring she is, how passionate and wise. But if I keep thinking that, I will be right back where I started.

I get up and follow her, trying to shed the weight of expectation as I go.

CHAPTER TWELVE
WENDY

There's no turning back.

Today is the day. Everyone who matters in Darkland will be attending our wedding this evening, and they will know, officially, that Roc belongs to James and me. And because I am a bit superstitious and didn't want to risk anything, I requested that we all spend our Wedding Eve in separate residences. Roc went back to his old loft in the Umbrage and rented James the King's Suite at a fancy hotel a few blocks south of the Dark Cathedral, where the wedding is to take place. They both decided it was safest for me to stay at Maddred Manor.

There has been a flurry of activity this morning. The staff made me the most beautiful breakfast spread, but I couldn't seem to eat a bite. I just sat there nursing my coffee, staring at the array of food while Asha ate next to me, chatting with our wedding planner, Yandall.

The nerves are getting the best of me.

Now in my dressing room in the west wing of the Dark Cathedral, Yandall and Asha are directing the makeup and hair people on how to style me, as we discussed weeks ago.

But my heart is racing and I feel sticky and hot.

"Wendy?" Asha is saying, but I feel faint.

"Give us a minute?" Asha says and everyone quickly exits the room.

"What's wrong?" she asks.

"What if I'm making the wrong decision?"

She pulls over one of the nearby stools and sits in front of me, taking my hand in hers. I'm not in my dress yet, just a silk robe, feet bare, but I think I might perish from heat stroke.

"If you want to call it off, I can arrange it," she says.

"What? No!" I catch on immediately. "You were testing me."

"Yes." She gives my hand a squeeze. "You countered me quickly. You barely had to think about it."

I blow out a breath. "Yes, I do want to marry them both. I just hope they want to marry me. Roc could be doing this for perception. He's got a reputation that is centuries old, so he has to clean it up. And James might be saying yes because he thinks it's what we want. But is it what he wants?"

"James is madly in love with both of you, so yes, I do."

"He is?"

Asha tilts her head. "Wendy Darling."

I deflate and close my eyes. "Okay. Okay. Clearly, my self-consciousness is getting in my way." I pop my eyes open again and look over at Asha, endlessly patient Asha. "Most of my life in the Seven Isles, I was only wanted for my power and what I could give. No one cared who I actually was, or what I actually wanted. I'm just scared, Asha."

"I know you are." She coaxes me up and embraces me deeply. "They love you. Both of them. Do not doubt that."

"And I love you to the bottom of my heart." I kiss the

side of her head, grateful to have her. "When I'm queen, can I please make you a duchess? And give you a beautiful manor on the sea full of old books and rolled scrolls to thank you for your tireless friendship?"

"Will it come with a sexy butler?"

"I'm sure we can drum one up."

She laughs and then calls the others back in and preparations for the wedding resume.

CHAPTER THIRTEEN
HOOK

Bloody hell. If I didn't love Wendy as much as I do, and if I had no vested interest in her continued happiness, I would not have agreed to her superstitions. We've been living together for months, but on the eve of our wedding, we're not allowed to see each other? For what reason? To avoid a catastrophe? Disaster will strike, superstition or not.

Roc rented me the finest room in The Dorian House, but I still found the bed sorely lacking in comfort and warmth. Or perhaps it was the emptiness of the bed. I've come to expect Wendy and Roc beside me at night and the sudden solitude bristled like a sea urchin.

It didn't help that the wine selection, while sensible, was not fine, and the food, while edible, was just mediocre. Our cooks have clearly ruined my taste for any other dining.

Because I tossed and turned half the night, I wake late for my own damn wedding and have to dash out of the hotel with no coffee and nothing to eat. Which is just as well. I don't relish the idea of standing at the altar and vomiting on Roc's shoes.

No, no, I will not vomit. I will not be nervous. I will not be a blustering ball of anxiety and—

I turn the next street corner, fighting with my hook, trying to get it latched on my arm, when I slam into someone. My hook is bumped off and it clatters down the sidewalk.

"Bloody fucking hell, you idiot! Watch where you're going!"

A pistol arm clicks as it's pulled back. A barrel is pointed at my nose.

"Keep your voice down," the man says, half his face hidden in the shadow of his wide-brimmed hat.

"I beg your pardon?"

"Into the carriage."

"I'm not—" I'm cut off when a glass bottle is thrust into my face and a cool mist sprays out, filling my nose with its acrid sweetness.

My vision swims and my ears ring.

I stagger to the side and several arms collect me, feet shuffling me forward.

"Get 'em into the carriage!" someone whispers.

"I'm fucking trying!" another says.

"Before someone sees!"

I can't feel my feet or my arms, and I'm buoyed up into a tottering carriage.

"Hey...unhand...me," I say, but the words come out garbled.

I'm dumped onto a bench. The world spins. I try to open my eyes, but my vision is ringed in black, and my eyes are watering.

"Shut the door!"

There's a loud slam. A thump. We lurch forward.

"I have a..." *wedding.* I can't get the word out.

I swing forward, trying to get myself free, but I roll off the bench.

Someone curses above me.

"Get the fogshade!"

Oh bloody hell. That's what they sprayed me with. A sleeping poison.

I swing again, but my head is still pounding, my vision still swimming. I'm fucking useless. Like a newborn fawn trying to get its feet beneath it.

Another burst of mist and the sweet, pungent elixir of the fogshade hits my senses, and instantly, I'm out.

What did I say?

Disaster will strike, superstition or not.

CHAPTER FOURTEEN
ROC

If you had told me in very recent history that one day I would be sharing a drink in the Joker's Den with my little brother, Vane, his Darling, Winnie, along with Peter Pan, and the fae princes, Kas, and Bash, I would have asked you: what am I wearing and do I look handsome?

I am, in fact, dazzling today.

No one wears a three-piece suit better than me, the Devourer of Men, AKA the Crocodile, AKA the future king of Darkland.

The Joker's Den is closed today in observance of my wedding, but we've gathered here for a celebratory pre-drink.

My bartender, Skinny Egg, as he is affectionately known because he's bald and skinny and looks like an egg, has poured us each a shot of bourbon. My favorite.

Sitting on my left is my brother, Vane. On my right is Kas, then Bash, Winnie and Peter Pan.

Peter Pan radiates power like a fucking inferno. At his request, all of the windows are drawn closed so the daylight can't reach him. He's a god, a primordial star, and he and the sun don't mix. He'll miss the wedding while day still reigns, but I've invited him to the after-party and made him promise not to outshine me. My jokes about stars notwithstanding, he seems to be tolerating me and my demands quite well.

I raise my glass. "To new alliances," I say.

They nod and lift their glasses and we all drink to that.

"Shall we toast to—"

The front of the Joker's Den bursts open.

Peter Pan curses and disappears in a flash of light.

Vane and the twins are on their feet.

I turn, a little bored, and spot Smee in the doorway.

"You aren't invited," I tell her.

Like Peter Pan, Smee tolerates me because of our overlapping interests. But she once hurt my feelings and I haven't forgiven her.

"Jas has been kidnapped," she says and comes into the main room, letting the door slam shut behind her.

I go very, very still. "He what?"

"I was meeting him at The Dorian House and caught sight of him as they were shoving him into a carriage."

Blood is rushing through my ears.

"Who are 'they'?"

"I don't know. I don't know your deplorables. But I have a description of the carriage."

I may be a Jabberwocky at my core, but taking on the Darkland Dark Shadow means I don't have access to my monster. But still, it writhes with that age-old need to devour.

To make those who cross me disappear.

"Who the fuck was stupid enough to kidnap the Crocodile's boyfriend?" Kas is saying.

"RIP to that guy," Bash adds.

My teeth grind together. I suck in a breath and try to quell the rage turning my vision red.

"Tell me everything you saw, Smee. And tell me quickly."

CHAPTER FIFTEEN
HOOK

I come to a little groggy, my head pounding.

I attempt to lift my hand to rub the blurriness from my eyes and find immediate resistance.

Blinking through the haze, I look down and realize I'm tied to a chair. My hook is gone.

And then it comes back to me—

Someone took me hostage and drugged me in their carriage.

As some of the haze wears off, I scan my surroundings but don't find much to pick out. The room is dark save for a naked, flickering bulb above me. The floor is cracked stone, dirty and damp. Licking my lips, I taste salty sea air and, somewhere behind me, a sharp breeze.

We must be near the water.

"Good, you're awake," someone says as they come around to face me.

There's a green mask tied around their nose and mouth, obscuring their features. Stitched on the front of the fabric are two snake eyes and a serpent tongue.

Bloody hell.

Gutter Snakes.

I vaguely recall Manuel telling me the Gutter Snakes were trying to bribe several of the workers in the Portage Hall so they could get some of their illegal shipments into the harbor. No one had taken the bait yet, and good on them.

Except now I seem to be paying the price.

The question is...did they take me hostage because I'm the portage minister or because I'm connected to the future King of Darkland?

If it's the latter, they might be the dumbest criminals to ever walk this island.

Two more men join the first. All three of them are wearing the matching masks of the Gutter Snakes. The first one is the shortest with a portly middle and a floppy cap on his head. The man on the left is tall and wiry, wearing a tweed jacket. The man on the right is stocky, wearing a plaid shirt with the sleeves rolled up.

"What the bloody hell is this?" I twist at the bindings, but they at least seem to know what they're doing with rope.

The man on the left, Tweed, whispers to the man in the middle, Shorty. "What happened to his hand?"

"What? How should I know?" Shorty whispers back.

"Did you cut it off?" Plaid asks.

"No!"

"You idiots."

A fourth voice rings out from the shadows and a woman steps in. She's wearing no mask, but her hair is tucked up into a newsboy cap. Her clothing, too, is purposefully baggy and masculine so she can hide any defining features.

"Where's his hand?" she repeats. "Who on this god forsaken island is missing a hand?"

The three men look at one another. Some realization starts to flicker in their eyes.

"Who is missing a hand and wears a…" She trails off, letting them put the pieces together.

"A hook," Shorty says.

Tweed widens his eyes. "Oh no."

Plaid doubles over, pulls down his mask and vomits on the stone.

"Holy shit. HOLY SHIT!" Tweed turns a circle, then runs away, then doubles back. "We're going to fucking die, eh! We're going to be dead by sundown!"

"How the fucking hell did you kidnap Captain Hook?" Shorty yells at no one. "It was supposed to be a page from the Portage Hall!"

"No, you said someone higher up!" Tweed shouts back. "Someone important!"

"I didn't say that!"

"Yes, you did!" Plaid yells, his voice wet and raw.

"Shut up. All of you," the woman says. She comes over to me and crosses her arms over her chest. "Captain Hook."

"That's me."

"There seems to have been a terrible mistake."

I snort. "You could say that."

"What do you say we let you go and forget this ever happened?"

"Back on Neverland, you all would be gutted for this kind of a mistake. How do you call yourselves a gang?"

The woman digs in her pants pocket and mist assaults my sinuses again.

The room sways.

"We need some time to figure out our next steps," she says. "I hope you don't mind."

"He's...going...to...k—" I don't finish my sentence before I'm out again.

CHAPTER SIXTEEN
WENDY

WHEN ROC INSISTS ON COMING INTO MY DRESSING ROOM IN THE
Dark Cathedral, just an hour before we are to walk down
the aisle, I know something must be wrong.

My heart is racing in my ears. This is it, I think. He's
changed his mind.

But when he pushes into the room, there's fury on his
face.

"What is it?"

"Someone has taken our Captain."

"What?" I shout, because I'm certain I misheard him.

Asha is beside me in an instant.

"We think it was the Gutter Snakes," Roc goes on. "They
had been paying Yal Mertz for port entry of stolen goods.
With Mertz gone, and Captain in charge, they haven't been
getting their way so I suspect they decided to take a
different route."

What he's saying makes sense on the surface. Hally
used to take bribes all the time to allow bad people to do
bad things in Everland.

But what doesn't make sense is that someone would be stupid enough to take James when he's...well, James Hook.

"So what are you going to do?" I ask.

"I'm going to go get him," he tells me matter-of-factly.

"I'm coming with you."

"No, you're not."

"Roc. You didn't come here to tell me James has been kidnapped, expecting me to sit down and wait patiently while you go get him. Did you?"

"Wendy," he says, sounding a little exasperated.

"I'll be her shadow," Asha says.

"And what Asha can't cover, I'm sure Hagan can," I say pointedly.

Roc raises a brow.

"What, you thought I wouldn't notice that our house manager is always watching my every move?"

"I had hoped you wouldn't, yes."

"Don't insult me like that ever again." I'm still in my silk robe and I didn't bring an extra set of clothing other than my wedding dress. I can't really run into a hostage situation wearing a robe.

"I have something for you," Asha says and unzips the bag she brought with. She pulls out a black outfit not unlike her usual attire. It's close-fitting and unassuming. It'll be perfect.

"Five minutes," Roc says. "And then we leave."

When Asha and I emerge through a side entrance of the cathedral, as Roc instructed, we're greeted by him, Vane, Winnie, Kas, Bash, and Smee. Peter Pan is missing but I'm assuming that's because the sun is still out.

I was confident in our odds when it was just me, Asha, and Roc. But with the rest of them? I almost feel sorry for these Gutter Snakes.

"Are we allowed to toss anyone off a cliff?" Bash asks, his wings fluttering behind him.

"No," Roc answers. "There's always a possibility someone could survive being tossed off a cliff."

"What are you thinking, then?" Vane asks his brother.

"Let's make their entrails into necklaces."

Vane steps forward. "We should be back in time for the wedding then."

"And then drinks!" Bash yells.

Oh gods. This new life I live is sometimes impossible to reckon with.

CHAPTER SEVENTEEN
ROC

It turns out, Skinny Egg knows exactly where I can find the Gutter Snakes and by the time the sun is touching the ocean's horizon line, we're circling the old dock warehouse.

The plan is simple: Asha and Wendy will go to the front door and knock and pretend to be lost.

Smee and I will sneak in through a side entrance.

Vane, Kas, Bash and Winnie will circle the place watching for any escapees.

Now, Smee and I are crouched behind a stack of empty crates in the lot on the east side of the warehouse. It gives us a clear view of the unmarked front entrance, where Asha and Wendy are currently approaching, along with the back entrance, where we plan to enter.

I originally wanted to smash my way inside and start tearing off limbs, but Smee pointed out that the Snakes could be holding my Captain at gunpoint and any smash and grab could risk his life.

So now I sit out here crouching behind refuse like a thief.

"When we get in," I tell Smee, "you should step aside. I will be tearing limbs from bodies."

She shifts slightly so she can peer around the corner of a crate. "Do you not know how to be discreet?"

"Subtlety has never been my strong suit."

Wendy and Asha are at the front door. Wendy reaches out with her fist and knocks.

They wait.

As a Jabberwocky, I had heightened senses and while the Darkland Dark Shadow has dulled some of the Jabberwocky elements, my senses were not one of them.

Inside the warehouse, I can hear shuffling of feet on stone and mumbling between several Gutter Snakes. They can't seem to decide who should answer the door.

Asha knocks a second time and Wendy calls out, "Hello? I'm looking for Mr. Killips?"

Finally, several locks on the front door are clunked open and someone peeks out.

I don't wait for Smee. Staying low, I hurry around the crates and to the back door. Smee is quick on my heels, a lock-picking set already in her hand.

"I don't need that, Smee," I tell her and turn the doorknob. Inside, the locks give easily. "Perks of having a shadow older than the dawn of time."

She rolls her eyes and then I shove inside.

CHAPTER EIGHTEEN
HOOK

When I come to again, I know exactly where I am and in what predicament.

I'm still tied to a chair. Still without a weapon. Still mostly in the darkness.

But there's a commotion somewhere behind me, in another room. And directly in front of me, a tiny spot of light.

My vision is still hazy and I squint, trying to make sense of its shape. It's about the size of a berry, but brighter than the sun. I can't look directly at it without my eyes burning.

Somewhere in the recess of the building, a lock is opened. Hinges creak.

And in front of me, another opened lock.

I know right away that Roc has arrived.

Maybe at this point I could sense him anywhere. In darkness or in light.

Then Wendy's voice rings out. "We're lost and hoped you could help. We're looking for Mr. Killips and we were given this address but—"

"There's no Killips here," Shorty says. "Can't help you."

"Sir, please!"

That's Asha.

More whispering beyond my hostage room. The voices are insistent, a little panicked.

"We should run," someone says. "Before the Crocodile devours us all!"

"Captain."

Roc's voice is like a balm on a burning wound.

I sigh and some of the tension fades from my spine.

He steps into the small ring of light dressed in his three-piece suit. His wedding attire.

What a way to start our union.

Behind him is Smee. She's not dressed for a wedding, but then she isn't one to put on a dress when a pair of leather trousers will do.

"Are you hurt?" Roc asks.

"They've knocked me out three times now. Or maybe two. I don't remember. My head is pounding."

More footsteps behind us and then someone enters the room. They come to a sudden stop with a collective breath.

Roc pops a cigarette in his mouth, cups his hand around the end as he puts it to flame. As he inhales, he turns his head up toward the naked bulb, all that sharp light glancing off his beautiful face.

The smoke curls up.

"I'm not sure what your motives are for this..."

The Gutter Snakes whisper to one another.

"And I don't care," Roc goes on. "Because in" —he pulls out his pocketwatch and flips open the lid— "less than six minutes, you will be dead."

The silence that hangs after his proclamation is heavy and still.

And then—

Shouting. Panic. The rustle of fabric and the land of hurried footfalls as they race to the front of the warehouse.

"I'll untie him," Smee says to Roc. "You go have your fun."

Roc holds the cigarette away and kisses me on the mouth. He tastes of rum and burning tobacco and relief.

It occurs to me that I haven't kissed him like this in front of Smee and for a half second, my face is hot and embarrassed until Roc pulls away and I spy Smee hiding a smile behind the back of her hand.

"I'm glad you're okay, Captain," Roc says. "I would have burned the place to the ground if they'd hurt you. Thank you, Smee," he adds, and then he's gone.

CHAPTER NINETEEN
ROC

I wish I could say I do not delight in the destruction of others.

But if you've wronged me or mine, I could throw a party dedicated to your dismemberment.

And I would for the Gutter Snakes if I didn't already have a party planned today, not in the honor of their spilled blood, but in the union of my love.

So I really must be hasty.

Before I took on the Darkland Dark Shadow, I would let my monster do the dirty work. And there was a separation between us that almost allowed me to believe the carnage was not mine to claim.

That is not the case now. And I don't want it to be.

The Dark Shadow writhes like a beast below dark waters, hungry to destroy.

There is no devouring this time. Just death.

I reach a man wearing a tweed jacket. He's the slowest, huffing and puffing to keep up with his friends. I yank him back by the scruff of his neck and he yelps as I break his neck.

More shouts sound from the front.

A door is slammed shut and barricaded.

"Let us out! Let us out!" they shout, but clearly Vane, Wendy and Asha and the others have done their work on the outside of the warehouse.

I take up a chunk of hair—man or woman, I don't know —and spin the person around. Man. I smash his face in. It's a beautiful blood bouquet.

He tries to scream but his mouth is full of blood so I smash him again and he is dead.

The Dark Shadow says yes, yes, make them pay.

And I gladly will.

Another man and a punch to the gut that breaks several ribs.

A man at the door, beating his fist against it. I kick downward, catching him behind the knee and his bones give like putty.

Someone shoots a gun and the bullet hits me in the back.

It hurts, sure, but the pain is distant and the shadow is fast to push the bullet back out.

I turn.

A blond man stands a few feet off, his hand shaking, holding a pistol.

I am impossible to kill.

But I'm impressed that he had the balls to try.

I dart across the room, tear the gun from his hand and accidentally tear his hand off with it. He howls, stumbles back on his ass while gripping his wrist, blood painting the air.

I take a step.

He scoots backward, whimpering. And when I stand over top of him, he pisses himself.

I disentangle his mutilated hand from the gun and toss it aside, where it flops, heavy and wet, on the stop.

I point it at him.

"Please. Crocodile. Please we made a mistake!"

I pull the trigger. The pop of the bullet seems to fill every hollow corner of the warehouse.

It hits him in the forehead, and he lies back, eyes wide and blank.

Behind me, a whimper.

I light a fresh cigarette with a hand painted red.

I follow the sound of the crying and find a girl cowering behind a stack of boxes.

"Oh god," she says.

"Not god," I answer and take another hit from my cigarette. "Your king."

She swallows, nods. "Your Majesty. I...we...they made a mistake."

I crouch in front of her. Her gaze takes in the sight of me.

I don't have a mirror but I can feel the blood dripping from my nose, from my chin.

"Tell them what you saw here. Spare no detail."

She nods. "I will. I promise. I'll tell everyone."

"Open the door," I shout and the barricade is removed. "Go on," I tell her.

She scurries to her feet and tears out of the warehouse, the door banging against the wall.

And I make a turn around the room, scanning what I have done.

This carnage? All of this is mine. And I am happy to claim it.

CHAPTER TWENTY
HOOK

"Smee? Do you see that ball of light over there?"

She undoes the bindings on my wrist and looks over her shoulder. And when she glances back at me, she's frowning. "No. Did they hit you on the head?" She pokes at my face, checking my eyes.

"No. Stop that. You don't see it?"

"No." She crouches in front of me and slices through the bindings on my ankles, freeing me from the chair.

I rub at my arm, keenly aware of the absence of my hook.

I'm not sure if I'll be able to recover it now, but I do have a spare at home, thank god.

When I stand, the light rises as if following my movements.

Smee still seems unaware of it.

Did I hit my head? Maybe I'm still fuzzy from the poison?

I don't feel fuzzy.

"Sounds like your boyfriend is taking out his rage on the

Gutter Snakes," Smee is saying, but I'm barely listening to the cries for help coming from the other room.

I take a step toward the light.

It zips upward, frenzied now.

There are myths of tiny fairies, but no one has seen them in centuries, if they were ever real in the first place.

The closer I get, the more I have to squint, the light is so bright.

When I'm just a few feet from it, the light starts vibrating and I have a moment to wonder if it's some kind of magical bomb about to blow, when suddenly it careens toward me, hitting me in the chest.

The force of the hit sweeps me off my feet and I fly backwards, arms pinwheeling.

But before I land on the stone floor, I'm out again.

CHAPTER TWENTY-ONE
WENDY

A woman, face glistening with tears, races out of the front of the warehouse. She doesn't look back and within seconds, she's disappeared around the next building.

Roc appears in the open door, a cigarette in his hand.

He's covered in blood. It's splattered over his face and it's turned his hands red.

This is the Roc I know well. The one more at home with carnage than deskwork.

There is the hint of a smile on his face.

"All is well, Wendy Darling," he calls. "But perhaps you should come in through the back door."

Asha and I share a look. One thing that could be said for Hally and the Everland Court is that most of their cruelty was psychological. I was spared from the gore of violence or war. Asha was not so lucky and I know she shielded me from it as much as possible.

I don't have a weak stomach, but it is my wedding day. So if I can avoid seeing limbs torn from bodies, I think I will gladly take it.

Vane, though, he goes in the front door to join his

brother, while Asha and I make our way around to the back of the warehouse where the others have gathered. Asha is in ahead of me, with the fae brothers bringing up the rear. In the late sunlight, their dark, pearlescent wings glitter like abalone shells.

Inside the warehouse, there's a short hallway that widens into a holding area.

When I come in, I find Smee crouched beside James, who is unconscious on the floor.

"What happened?" I race to him and drop to the floor. He's breathing, thank the gods, and I don't see any wounds.

"He kept talking about seeing a light, and then all of a sudden he was knocked off his feet," Smee tells me as she undoes some of the buttons on his shirt. "He was unconscious when he landed. So it wasn't the fall that knocked him out."

She runs her hands over his chest, then over the back of his neck and his shoulders. "I don't feel anything broken or swollen. They did use fogshade on him so it could be—"

James gasps and lurches upright. "Bloody hell!" He grasps at his chest, tearing his shirt open as if searching for something. "Where did it go?"

"Where did what go?" I ask.

"I think he's talking about the light," Smee says, and as she says it, her expression changes, her mouth popping open, her eyes widening.

"What? What is it?" I ask.

Smee pokes at James's face, checking his eyes.

"Smee! Stop doing that!"

"What did this light look like?" she asks, pulling up his eyelid. He bats her away.

"It was tiny. Like the size of a berry. Dense and bright. It hit me." He presses his fingers to his sternum. The skin is unmarred. No bruising, no burns. Nothing.

The twins come into the room. Bash's wings pull inward, folding against his body as he sits on an overturned crate. His brother stands beside him, arms crossed. And then I hear the faint tinkling of bells.

I know that some fae can speak to each other in a language no one else can understand, and when they do, it sounds like the chiming of bells.

"What are you two saying?" Smee asks.

"Oh, nothing," Bash answers with a grin.

"Kas," Smee says.

Kas is about to answer when Vane and Roc come into the room.

"Time is ticking," Vane says, a pocketwatch open in his hand. "We have seventeen minutes to get back to the cathedral and to the wedding. I have a carriage waiting for those of you stuck on the ground."

He means me and James. The rest of them, even Roc now that he has the Darkland Dark Shadow, can fly.

"I'll ride with you two," Roc says as he drops his cigarette on the stone floor and crushes it beneath his boot. "I'm not taking any chances."

CHAPTER TWENTY-TWO
HOOK

We're well outside the Harbor District now, but because the carriage Vane summoned has none of the royal insignia, we're repeatedly getting stuck in traffic and time is ticking away.

Warmth is pulsing through my chest and I'm having a hard time sitting still in the carriage.

I keep pressing on my chest, making sure everything is as it should be. Is my heart about to explode? Am I losing my damn mind?

I sigh and rub at my eyes, and when I look across the carriage next, I find Roc staring at me.

His gaze is penetrating, like he's searching for something.

"What?" I ask.

"You seem different."

"I was just kidnapped."

He blows out a breath. "You're a pirate. Surely you've been kidnapped before?"

There was that one time we ran into a rival crew in the back streets of Summerland and I was taken hostage in exchange for gold. And again, years later, when a witch hunter took me captive, claiming I was an abomination. Smee and my crew had to rescue me.

Though now that I think of it, I suppose the hunter had a point. I had Myth Maker magic running through my veins. I didn't know that at the time. I'm shocked I survived that one. Witch hunters are brutal and they rarely fail at their jobs.

"I'm fine," I tell Roc even though I don't feel fine.

Not that I feel bad, either.

Just...*okay*, yes, *different*.

Traffic clears and the carriage lurches forward. Beside me, Wendy is quiet.

This isn't how any of us wanted our wedding day to transpire.

Bloody Gutter Snakes.

Did they truly think kidnapping someone from the Portage Hall would get them what they wanted? It was ill-advised at best, downright suicidal at worst.

Wendy reaches over and takes my hand in hers. Nervous energy is pulsing through her and—

I glance over. She's staring out the carriage window, watching the city pass us by.

She is nervous. I know it in an instant, but...she's not fidgety. She's not biting her nails or worrying at her lip or any of the telltale signs of agitation.

So why would I think otherwise?

I look down at our hands intertwined. Her delicate fingers, the oval cut of her nails and it's like I can feel every-thing she's feeling in an instant.

I yank my hand away, and the sensation is gone.

Wendy turns sharply toward me. "What's wrong? Are you hurt?"

"No, I...my hand fell asleep, is all." The lie comes out before I can think better of it. I don't like dishonesty between us, but I've already contributed too much chaos to our day of union. I won't contribute more.

I must be feeling the aftereffects of the fogshade.

I can sense Roc's attention lingering on me like a slant of warm sunlight.

But this time, I pretend not to notice.

CHAPTER TWENTY-THREE
WENDY

The carriage ride back to the cathedral seemed to take eons and we technically arrive before our wedding is scheduled to begin, but now I have to redress and when Roc parted ways, he was still covered in blood and viscera, and James was still missing his hook.

Now, I'm pacing my dressing room, hands wringing. I'm half-dressed and fully freaking out. I dismissed everyone other than Asha because I can't take being perceived right now. I am not acting queenly. Not in the slightest. I feel like a frightened little girl.

Asha comes in from the adjoining room and hands me a white ceramic mug. There's a dark liquid inside, steam rising from the surface.

"It'll help calm the nerves," she tells me and I don't have to hear any more.

I take the cup and appreciate its warmth and Asha's kindness, but the scent is pungent and overwhelming. And I know immediately what it is. "Valerian?" I ask her.

"Yes. But there's also lavender, chamomile, and honey. It smells worse than it tastes."

I'm only slightly dubious, but I could use all of the calming medicine I can get, so I take a sip. She isn't wrong. The other flavors help mask the valerian's undertones of damp wood.

"Did Roc get changed?" I ask.

Asha nods. "And a delivery boy just arrived with James's hook. All is well."

I exhale and finally drop into a nearby chair. "Maybe it will still go off without issue?"

"Are you concerned about issues?" she asks.

"Anything other than perfection will be perceived as a bad omen."

"Will it?"

I sigh. "You weren't there for my wedding to Hald. Right before I was to say, 'I do,' one of the glass candle holders shattered. I was ostracized from court for months with gossip swirling around our union, how I must have cursed him or put a spell on him, followed by the even more insane rumor that I was a witch trying to overthrow the entire kingdom."

"Yes, but that was in Everland and you were forced into that marriage. You are choosing this. No matter what happens, this time, it will be different."

I take another sip of the tea and let the warmth soothe my frazzled nerves.

I just hope Asha is right.

My heart is racing.

The wedding ballad is playing from the giant organ set at the heart of the church. Darkland's wedding ballad is haunting, almost melancholy, and it makes me immediately emotional.

Tears burn at my eyes.

I'm doing this. I don't care what bad omens say about any of this. I love Roc and I love James and I can't imagine going back to a life without them.

I'm waiting in the west wing for my cue to enter. Asha is just behind me and to the right. Darkland wedding tradition calls for each party to have a witness. Asha was a no-brainer, though I do feel slightly guilty that I was unable to add a second and have Winnie join. She assured me she had no hard feelings and that whoever was by my side should be my very best friend and we had only just recently met, pointing out that it was Asha who had been by my side for every major life event and that this one should be no different.

Truly, it was kind of her to insist and absolve me of my guilt, and yet it remains.

Vane is standing for Roc and Smee is standing for James.

If all has gone according to plan, the four of them will be waiting for me on the dais. Roc on the left, James on the right, with space held for me in the middle.

The wedding ballad finally hits my cue and I take a deep breath, leave the shadows of the west wing behind, and walk down the aisle.

CHAPTER TWENTY-FOUR
HOOK

It feels like everyone who is anyone in Darkland is staring at me, silently judging me. I don't belong up here standing as an equal with the Duke of Maddred and future king. I'm sure they're all wondering how I conned my way here. And similarly, trying to figure out how to be rid of me. At least if they were left with Wendy, she would have the grace, etiquette, and experience to rule by Roc's side.

Bloody hell why is it so hot in here?

Calm down. Calm down. All will be well. You deserve to be up here.

But do I? Do I??

I clasp my hook behind my back with my other hand in an effort to ward off any fidgeting.

My pulse is racing, my lungs feel starved of air, and this collar feels too fucking tight around my neck.

The wedding ballad shifts in tempo and I know that's Wendy's cue to start her procession down the aisle.

I stare straight ahead as those seated in the pews turn to watch the future queen of Darkland enter the church.

And with their attention directed elsewhere, some of the tension ebbs out of my bones.

I take a deep breath and refocus and there she is.

Wendy Darling is radiant in her wedding dress.

It's styled in the Darkland style with the bodice made of black lace, with a large white skirt of satin and several gauzy layers of black overtop. Her dark hair is curled and pinned back, exposing her pale shoulders and the delicate column of her neck where a solitary diamond hangs from a silver chain. Matching diamonds hang from her ears. But it's the giant diamond on her ring finger that catches my eye.

Our wedding ring. The setting is silver with a ring of tiny black diamonds around a large cut diamond in the center. Roc and I designed it together just days after we all said yes to his proposal. He and I have matching silver bands with three tiny black diamonds set into the silver, symbolizing the three of us. But because he took my left hand, mine rests on the ring finger of my right. And because Roc has begun to prove he is thoughtful, he decided to forgo tradition as well and wears his on his right.

We all went back and forth on how we wanted the ceremony to go, whether we wanted to put rings on each other during the ceremony, as is tradition, or perhaps just Roc and I put a ring on Wendy's finger. Ultimately, we decided to use a ribbon binding tradition from Wonderland, Roc's homeworld.

Wendy makes her way down the aisle and all of the Darkland elite watch her as if she is a fire burning brightly in the dark.

No one can question whether or not she belongs here. In some ways, I think she embodies power the most.

My eyes start to mist and heat rises up my throat. I don't want to be a blubbering fool up here.

But she's so beautiful. And Roc is so...Roc. And I am so grateful and lucky, it almost seems unreal.

When Wendy reaches the dais, Asha straightens out the long train of her gown and takes her place beside Smee.

The music fades out.

I can hear nothing over the heavy thump of my heart in my ears.

The officiant, Dominie Reeta, clears her throat and smooths out the pages of her book on the podium. When she speaks, her voice booms out.

"You are all gathered here today..."

Heat builds in my extremities and rushes through my veins. I keep licking my lips, trying to stave off the dryness of my mouth. I have to speak soon. I have to say, "I do," and I have to say it so everyone can hear it and...

I refocus and realize the officiant is already onto the second part and we're about to fasten hands.

Poor form, Jas! Poor fucking form!

Pay attention to your own fucking wedding.

Roc, Wendy and I are to move closer together so that we can link our hands and the officiant can fasten them with a black, silk ribbon. As we practiced it, Roc was to put his hand out first, then Wendy's, with mine on top, to symbolize our commitment to protecting her always and forever.

Wendy's hand is out first and Roc joins her, his hand placed beneath hers.

I step closer, every movement feeling clumsy and awkward.

I manage not to trip or fall and get my hand over top of Wendy's, but because hers is so small compared to ours, my hand covers hers completely, my fingers brushing against Roc.

The officiant steps forward, the long ribbon draped over her arms. She starts winding, tying us together, reciting the final binding words.

"With this ribbon, I bind thee," she says.

Heat rises up my arm.

"...in heart, mind, and soul, you are one."

Tingling starts in my fingers, spreading through my forearm, then up and up to my neck.

"Those who bear witness, I now pronounce Wendy Darling, James Hook, and Bane Maddred bound till death do them part."

The tingling floods my entire body. Then an overwhelming rush of emotion.

Excitement. Happiness. Eagerness. Fear. Solace. Anxiety.

I am immediately aware that not all of these emotions are mine.

I look up at Roc and Wendy in panic.

What is happening?

My vision tunnels, pulsing like a star and ringed in bright white light.

Roc frowns at me. Wendy's mouth pops open.

Something is wrong.

The officiant steps back, eyes wide.

Energy races up my spine, somehow hot and cold at the same time.

And then I'm pulling away, and the ribbon unwinds, trailing like an anchor line.

I'm off my feet, rising toward the soaring, domed ceiling high above.

"What...is...happening?" I shout, my voice echoing through the church.

The crowd murmurs and gasps.

On the left, I spot the twins and they're cajoling one another like they've won a bet.

"What is going on?" I shout again, my arms pinwheeling. I'm floating off, unable to get my feet beneath me. If I drop now, I'm dead.

"Congratulations, Captain Hook!" Kas shouts.

"You're one of us now!" Bash adds.

"What the bloody—how do I get down?"

"Does he have a shadow?" someone asks.

"He's flying without wings, he must!" another voice rings out.

I'm nearly at the curved iron beams holding the glass ceiling in place. Will I fly straight through?

The air whistles below me and a dark silhouette approaches.

Roc comes to a sudden stop in front of me, grabbing me by the hand, yanking me down before I reach the ceiling.

"Captain," Roc says.

"I don't know what's happening," I admit.

"I know."

"I didn't do this!"

"I know."

"I don't—"

He presses his mouth to mine, swallowing my objections.

Every time he touches me, something in me unwinds and lies flat.

I kiss him back, holding on to him for dear life.

When he pulls away and I open my eyes, I realize we're back on the ground, both feet on the floor.

I expel a breath of relief and turn to the church, thinking maybe I imagined it all. Maybe I blacked out during our vows and—

Everyone in attendance rises from their seats and then sinks to their knees in deference.

"What is this?" I ask Roc.

"Well, Captain," he says and clasps his hands behind his back, "traditionally speaking, in the Seven Isles, whoever possesses an island's Life Shadow is king."

My vision sways.

My stomach churns.

Bloody hell.

CHAPTER TWENTY-FIVE
ROC

For most of my life, I have watched men chase power like a shiny object glittering on the horizon.

There was never enough power, no matter how much they possessed. If they had all the power, they wanted more. All the land, the money, the titles, however much they could get, they wanted to call it theirs.

Rarer was seeing a man who hated power in possession of so much of it, it vibrated on the air.

Currently, I am staring at one such man, and lucky for me, he is mine.

As much as Captain James Hook likes to believe he is a cutthroat pirate, at the heart of it, he is just a big gooey cinnamon cake who wants to be loved and accepted for who he is. But more than that, he wants to feel worthy.

He's already told me seven times in seven different ways that he didn't intend to take the Darkland Life Shadow, that he never coveted it, that we should figure out how to get it out of him, proving to me that the shadow chose him for exactly this reason.

Because he does not covet this power.

It is that reason that he now glows with it.

And yet, he is trying to reassure me again. "There must be a way," he's saying to me and Wendy.

It's been hours since our vows were sealed, since we were announced husband and husband and wife.

The Captain tried to avoid the public spectacle of stepping out as the one now in possession of the shadow, but there was no way I was going to let him off the hook so easily. Pun intended? Of course.

We're in the ballroom in the Darkland Palace. Wendy is in the middle, between us. All of the Darkland elite is in attendance, most of them fast approaching drunkenness.

"James," Wendy starts, but I cut her off.

"Captain. Do you think I'm upset?"

"Aren't you?"

I'm a little offended that he can't tell. Does he not know me? Body and soul?

"Why would I be?"

"You're meant to be the most powerful," he says matter-of-factly.

"So you cannot be powerful too?"

Wendy takes his hand in hers and squeezes. But he carries on.

"You're to be king. I would never try to undermine you!"

I can sense the shadow pulsing beneath his skin. If he's not careful, he will float away again.

How I missed this change in the warehouse, and the carriage ride to the palace, is beyond me. I was still riding the high of killing those who thought they could take him from me. So I was a little distracted, I suppose.

Wendy reaches over and takes my hand too, linking us all together. It dawns on me that she may also be feeling alienated now that the Captain and I both have shadows. But if she does, she's not portraying it.

Wendy is much like the Captain—power does not attract her. I think there is a little part of her that enjoys the adventure of magic and prestige, sure. But abandon all else for it? Not Wendy Darling. She's too rational for that.

"This is my wedding day," Wendy says to both of us. "I will never get this day back. So if we want to discuss rank and power and shadows, let us discuss it tomorrow? Hmm?"

"Of course, Darling." I lean in and plant a kiss on her cheek and then smirk at the Captain because in a way I've gotten exactly what I wanted.

He frowns, but squeezes Wendy's hand and then kisses the back of her knuckles. "I will do whatever you ask, love."

"Thank you." She smiles at both of us, her eyes glittering. "More than anything, I want to survive this ball so that I can have you both in my bed tonight. And you may both have shadows, and you may both need to discuss who is actually king, but there was never any question about my role. I am your queen and tonight you will treat me as such."

I let out a low whistle. "Wendy Darling, you make me hard when you talk like that."

She demurs, but there is pride in her gaze. "Save it for later."

"Oh Darling, you have my word."

CHAPTER TWENTY-SIX
WENDY

BY THE TIME THE GUESTS HAVE GONE AND WE ARE ALONE IN THE Darkland Palace, all three of us are terribly drunk.

I stumble into our bedroom first fighting with the zipper on my dress. Laughter is bubbling up my throat, fizzing like champagne on the tip of my tongue. I can't even remember what I'm laughing at, but it doesn't matter. It just feels good.

Now that our wedding is over, I finally feel like I can breathe and relax. I didn't realize until after the event just how much I had been holding myself back trying to make sure everything was in place, that I was making the right decision, and that all of us were in alignment.

Work still needs to be done (even more so now that James has one of two Darkland shadows) but that's the reality of any relationship.

Right now, I just want to sink into this warm, fuzzy feeling running through my veins and then fuck the shit out of my two men.

Roc helps me with my zipper as James pulls the drapes

closed and lights the dozen white candles set out on the dresser.

The mood in the room immediately changes. I have been waiting for this night for weeks and my heart is racing at the anticipation of it.

I promised Roc I would prepare myself for both of them and I think I've done my part.

With the zipper open, my dress slips off my shoulders and with a little wiggle of my hips, it falls off my body, pooling on the hardwood floor.

Both of my men take in the sight of me in the lingerie I took great care to select.

It was designed and hand-sewn by an artist in the Umbrage who I have become slightly obsessed with.

The piece is a black lace halter body suit that makes me feel like the sultry whore James accused me of being. But I'm not shying away from it. Not now, not ever. In fact, I want to embrace it. Because every time I brush up against the darker parts of myself, or the taboo desires that society, especially Everland, told me I should not have, I feel like a god.

"Bloody hell," James says.

"Wendy Darling." Roc comes to stand in front of me and looks me up and down. "You've been wearing that under your wedding dress all day and you didn't tell us?" He tsk-tsks.

"If I'd told you, it wouldn't have been a surprise."

"And you wouldn't have gotten through the vows," James says to him.

Roc hooks his arm around James's shoulders and drags him into his side. "You have a point, husband."

The smile that pulls at James's mouth is instinctual, almost giddy. "Husband."

Roc runs his fingers through James's hair. "Husband. Wife. Husband. What a delight this is."

I cross the distance between us and start unbuttoning Roc's shirt. And as I do, Roc trails a hand down my arm, then down my torso. A shiver wracks my body.

When I finally get his shirt open and get to take in the full sight of his stomach and all the ink that swirls over his chest, heat burns in my cheeks.

"I will never stop marveling at how hot you are," I tell him.

"Oh Wendy, Darling, stop. You're making me blush."

James snorts. "You, bashful? Tell me more lies."

Roc reaches over and grips James by the groin. James groans. "Another lie? All right, Captain." He turns his body toward James and strokes him through his pants. "I will be patient with you tonight."

James blows out a breath, his eyes slipping closed. "A lie I am happy to swallow then."

"You'll be swallowing more than that."

I think some people might feel left out, watching the dynamics play out between Roc and James, but I consider it foreplay. Because what Roc promises James, I know he promises me, too.

"Christ." James huffs out a breath. "You may be the end of me."

Roc laughs and then kisses James. The kiss is slow and attentive. My heart races in my chest.

Watching them, my mouth goes parched, and I draw my tongue over my lips, wetting them, and the wet smack of my lips draws Roc back.

When he refocuses his gaze on me, lust burns in his eyes.

"Come here, Darling," he says and I sink into his side, curling my body against his.

He feels so good. All of this feels so good and right.

I'm treated to an echoing kiss, his tongue meeting mine.

And then suddenly I'm swept off my feet, cradled in Roc's arms. A surprised yelp escapes me and I wrap my arms around his neck as another burble of laughter escapes me.

"Captain," he calls, but James is already sliding onto the bed, positioning himself against the wall of thick pillows propped against the headboard. He spreads his legs so that Roc can nestle me into the space between them.

"You smell delightful, Darling," James says at the shell of my ear.

"Mmm," Roc says. "Fuckable and so, so sweet."

Butterflies dip in my belly as Roc climbs on the bed next and sinks down to his belly, his face now inches from my sensitive center.

I'm already dripping wet. I've been wet most of the day thinking about tonight, about being the wife to these two handsome, powerful, dangerous men, and all the things they will do to me tonight and every night that stretches on after it.

Roc breaths out and the heat penetrates the thin lace covering my pussy.

I moan and wiggle, feeling the hardness of James's cock pressing between my shoulders.

I want to be touched. I want to be teased. I want this night to last forever.

James reaches beneath my thigh with his hook, gently placing the tip against my skin, coaxing me open for Roc.

The way they move together, pleasuring me, I can't help

but wonder if I've made a deal with the devil to get this lucky.

Roc brushes his finger over the seam of my bodysuit, where my thigh meets my core, purposefully teasing me, touching me but not touching the aching parts.

I squirm again and James applies more pressure with his hook sending a sharp slant of pain through me, forcing me still.

"Patience, Wendy Darling," Roc says.

"But I thought you said you would not be patient." My argument comes out breathy and a little whiny.

"I will not be patient with our Captain. But you on the other hand…"

He drags his knuckles over my pussy and when I jolt beneath him, James captures my wrist in his hand, pulling me back, opening me up to both of them.

James plants a kiss on my neck, then my cheek as Roc plants a kiss at my clit, still keeping the delicate lace between us.

I breathe out, close my eyes, and sink into the feel of them.

I am so greedy for more.

Letting go of my arm, James finds my pebbled nipple and caresses it with the pad of his thumb.

And then Roc shoves aside the lace and runs his tongue over my pussy.

The moan that comes out of my throat is eager and high-pitched.

I'm already buzzing. I could come in a flash.

"Oh my god. Roc. Careful. I—"

But he is not careful and it turns out, also not patient.

The pleasure builds fast and hot and Roc doesn't let up. He hooks his hands around my thighs, holding me open as he devours me, tipping me over the edge before I have a chance to stop him.

I buck through the orgasm and James holds me to him, his hands roaming my body as shivers pound through me.

Eyes closed, I savor the pleasure, all of the tension running out of me.

But then the bed dips as Roc rises up and edges closer. And when I open my eyes next, I find Roc hovering over both of us, his trousers unbuttoned and hanging open, his hard cock bobbing between us.

Roc threads his fingers into James's hair and pulls him forward. "Not patient," he says, and then shoves his cock into James's mouth.

Roc groans, rocking his hips forward. "Captain, when I'm buried in your mouth, I feel closer to god."

I quickly adjust my position and run my tongue over the underside of Roc's shaft every time he pulls out.

"Fuck," he says, increasing his tempo as if chasing the pleasure of us both. "The desire to spill down your throat, the restraint needed not to."

He pulls out, chest heaving.

"Your Majesty," he says. "Have you done your homework?"

I wipe the wetness from my chin. "Yes."

"Then give me your ass." He yanks me around and tears through the delicate lace of the bodysuit, baring me for him. "Captain."

"You're sure, Darling?" he asks.

"Yes. Don't make me wait any longer, James."

A bottle of fairy oil is procured and when Roc presses the head of his cock to my backside, the oil is warm and slippery.

James needs no such assistance. I'm already dripping

down my thighs and the head of his cock slides into my pussy with no resistance.

I wrap my leg around his hip and bend my back for Roc, finding the right position to take them both.

Roc finds the right angle, slipping in an inch and I groan around him, feeling so full I could burst.

"Be gentle," James tells Roc and Roc says, "Wendy Darling, do you want me to be delicate with your tight little ass?"

My eyes are heavy, my desire potent, and when I look up at James, I find a worried knot between his brows. I drag my nails over the nape of his neck and he shivers beneath my touch, some of the worry fading.

"Don't be gentle with me. Either of you."

James exhales and I can feel the answering excitement throbbing through his cock.

Roc wraps his arm around me, his hand coming to my throat as he sinks in another inch.

"I want her to be sore tomorrow, Captain. I want her body to remember the feel of us."

"Her husbands," James says.

"Her kings," Roc answers.

A thrill races through me. "Yes."

"Let's fuck her senseless." Roc plants a kiss on my bare shoulder. "And fill her with so much cum it drips from every hole."

"Bloody hell," James says on a breath.

"Oh gods," I say as the promise of his words builds pressure in my clit again.

If this is the start of our marriage, I think I will be a happy and satisfied wife.

Roc presses his hips forward, burying himself further.

James does the same until they're both sunk inside of me, filling me up.

I could come just like this. Every nerve is pulsing with need.

They pull out, and sink back in, finding a rhythm together, fucking me together.

"Oh fuck," I say. The pressure builds and builds. This time the pleasure is fuller, faster, like the orgasm is building not just at my core, but somewhere deep down, on a soul level.

I cling to James, he clings to me, and Roc is touching us both, his hand on my hip, his other threading through James's hair.

And together, we climb higher and higher and higher and then we're soaring, our pleasure loud and primal.

My men rock into me, spilling inside of me, and I jolt against them both, buzzing from the aftershock of so much pleasure it makes my eyes burn.

I heave out a breath.

Roc sinks deep inside of me and holds himself there as if prolonging his own pleasure. James plants a kiss on the tip of my nose.

"I love you both so much," I whisper.

"I didn't know what love was until you two," James confesses.

Roc is silent for a beat. "I was terrified of love until you two." He runs his fingers over James's hair, then does the same to me, tucking a stray lock behind my ear. "I am terrified no more."

I sink into the sensation of being sated and content.

And before long, I'm out.

EPILOGUE
ROC

Two Months Later

I am crowned a week after our wedding. And because the Captain is now in possession of the Darkland Light Shadow, I demand he be crowned King Regent. The Darkland High Chamber has no objections to it, and even if they did, I doubt they'd voice them.

There is much work to be done, but I promised Wendy and the Captain that I would take some time off for a honeymoon and while it took nearly two months to find a window of freedom, I am now making good on my promise.

The Captain and I are lounging on a tufted bed on the back patio of a newly purchased house on the northern cliffs of Darkland. It's to be our summer home. The air here is cleaner, crisper. My sister Lainey used to love spending time by the sea and it makes me think fondly of her.

I am shirtless, the sun warming my skin.

The Captain is beside me, propped up against a mountain of pillows reading a book about monsters and men.

"Pay attention to me," I tell him.

"I'm reading," he says.

"Stop reading."

He sighs and sets the book aside and sinks down beside me. Something in him has come to rest since our wedding night. I think he still sometimes worries that all of this will pop and bleed, but I'm not going anywhere and I don't think Wendy is either, so he's stuck with us and I will prove it to him day after day.

I tangle my body with his and he lets me.

"Where is our Darling?" I ask.

"She said she was going to the bathroom but that was a while ago."

"Should we go in and find her?"

"I'm sure she just got distracted."

"Maybe." I close my eyes, enjoying the warmth of the sun and the warmth of the Captain's body against mine.

"Has she seemed...different?" I ask him.

He thinks for a moment. "Yes. Actually."

"Theories?"

"Maybe she's tired of our shit."

"Maybe she's overwhelmed by our handsomeness."

He snorts. "Your ego knows no bounds."

"The only way I prefer it."

A door on the back of the house creaks open.

"Speak of the Darling..." I say.

She comes around the patio and stops at the end of the tufted bed. She's wearing a white summer dress that billows in the sea breeze. She looks radiant. More so than usual.

"Wendy Darling," I say. "Where did you disappear to?"

There is a trembling smile on her face. "I need to tell you something. Both of you."

There is a serious bend to her words even though she's bursting with excitement.

I pull myself upright. "I'm listening."

She clamps her mouth shut and sucks in several deep breaths through her nose. I can hear the rapid thump of her heart over the pounding of ocean waves.

"What is it?" the Captain says, concern evident in his tone of voice.

"I'm pregnant."

We are silent for several long seconds.

Wendy clasps her hands together. "Say something!"

A thousand thoughts are running through my head. Is it mine? Is it James's? It's probably James's but it doesn't matter because it will be mine regardless. I will make a shit father but I will do everything in my power to be better than the day before.

I think of the family I have lost and the family I have gained and...am I crying?

Yes, yes I think I'm crying.

I look over at James, his mouth hanging open. "Congratulations, Captain."

"Me? But we don't know..." He takes a breath. "Congratulations to all three of us." He gets up and wraps Wendy in a hug. I climb from the bed, and do the same, both of us drowning her in our arms.

"You will make a radiant mother," I tell her.

"I love you both," she says through tears. "But I'm so scared."

"Surely between the three of us, we'll get something right?" I say.

We laugh together, the sun sinking toward the horizon.

I am hundreds of years old.

But it is now, in this moment, that I feel like my life has finally begun.

?

TTHANK YOU SO MUCH FOR READING THIS LITTLE TREAT installment in the Devourer series! I truly did not mean to write this book. I wrote the first chapter as a bonus scene for Substack (you should subscribe so you don't miss out on future bonuses!) and loved the thought of what came after. And if you've read Dark & Darker Still, then you can see how that ending began in this ending!

As far as I know, this is the last installment for Roc, Hook, and Wendy, but I will never say never and certainly never say no to a little bonus scene or two in the future if inspiration strikes.

Substack is the best place to stay up to date and hear about exclusive opportunities to join in the book fun.

Become a member for free here: https://nikkistcrowe.-substack.com/

ALSO BY NIKKI ST. CROWE

DEVOURER DUOLOGY

Devourer of Men

Devour the Dark

Devour the Snake

VANE & ROC ORIGIN STORY

Dark & Darker Still

VICIOUS LOST BOYS SERIES

The Never King

The Dark One

Their Vicious Darling

The Fae Princes

WRATH & RAIN TRILOGY

Ruthless Demon King

Sinful Demon King

Vengeful Demon King

Wrath & Reign Omnibus

HOUSE ROMAN

A Dark Vampire Curse

MIDNIGHT HARBOR

Hot Vampire Next Door: Season One

Hot Vampire Next Door: Season Two

Hot Vampire Next Door: Season Three

Hot Vampire Next Door: Season Four

Hot Vampire Next Door: Season Five

Secrets Drenched in Blood (Midnight Harbor Omnibus)

Bonus Scene Anthology

Ink & Feathers

ABOUT THE AUTHOR

NIKKI ST. CROWE is a *USA Today* Bestselling Author of several romantasy novels, including the #1 Amazon Bestselling Series, *Vicious Lost Boys*.

When not writing about villains getting the girl, and the girl getting the power, Nikki can be found with her husband and daughter on the shores of Lake Michigan hunting for the perfect sunset.

VISIT NIKKI ON THE WEB AT:
www.nikkistcrowe.com

www.ingramcontent.com/pod-product-compliance
Lightning Source LLC
Chambersburg PA
CBHW020042310726
48970CB00007B/2377